THE *Illegitimate* PRINCE

empi baryeh

Empi Baryeh

First Published in Great Britain in 2021 by
LOVE AFRICA PRESS
103 Reaver House, 12 East Street, Epsom KT17 1HX
www.loveafricapress.com

Text copyright © Empi Baryeh, 2021

ISBN: 978-1-914226-16-8
Also available in ebook format

ROYAL HOUSE OF SAENE

THE PRINCESSES:

His Defiant Princess by Nana Prah
His Inherited Princess by Empi Baryeh
His Captive Princess by Kiru Taye

THE PRINCES:

The Torn Prince by Zee Monodee
The Resolute Prince by Nana Prah
The Tainted Prince by Kiru Taye
The Illegitimate Prince by Empi Baryeh
The Future King by Kiru Taye

BLURB

Financier, Kalahari Asanti, specialises in corporate takeovers, but his next conquest is personal. The Kingdom of Bagumi owes him a great debt, one he intends to collect from King Ibrahim Saene, the father he's never met and the man he holds responsible for his mother's death.

Princess Edina Dampare is to be engaged and trying to accept the undeniable truth—no man will ever reach her on the same level as the stranger who imprinted on her soul when she wantonly yielded her innocence to him the one forbidden night she allowed herself to put desire before duty.

Kal's quest for revenge brings him face-to-face with the woman who's been haunting his dreams for the past eight months. Now the man who grew up with nothing is determined to reclaim everything the Royal House of Saene took from him...including her.

DEDICATION

For my dad. I miss you every day.

AUTHOR'S NOTE

Dear Reader,

I am thrilled to bring you my second contribution to the Royal House of Saene series.

In *The Illegitimate Prince*, Kalahari Asanti visits the kingdom of Bagumi seeking revenge on its ruler, King Ibrahim Saene, the father he's never met and the man he blames for his mother's death. He encounters the one woman he hasn't been able to forget since one magical night with her eight months earlier. She becomes a part of his plot to claim what's rightfully his, but being with her comes at a cost he might not be willing to pay...

In many ways, Kalahari is different from all the heroes I've written about. His story has been the toughest to write so far, but the experience also makes him one of my favourite heroes.

I hope you enjoy his story.

Connect with me on Facebook (empibaryeh), twitter (@empibaryeh), Instagram (empibaryeh) or visit my website (empibaryeh.com).

Empi

CHAPTER ONE

New Year's Eve.
8 months earlier ...
"You should have been a prince."

Kalahari 'Kal' Asanti stilled at the words—words so similar to those his mother had uttered on several occasions; words he'd learnt at an early age to dismiss as the romanticism of a woman who, despite the hand life had dealt her, had still believed in fairy tales. Unfortunately for his *Mamaa*, she didn't get the happily-ever-after she'd never stopped believing in. Even on her death bed when the irrefutable truth had laid bare the lie she'd stubbornly clung to all these years, she'd played her final card and revealed a secret she should have taken to her grave.

The truth had unleashed venom into Kal's heart and set him on a path of vengeance. Instead of the tearful reunion she'd hoped for, his mother had ensured the downfall of the man she claimed to love.

She had one thing right, though. He was indeed going to meet the Saene family of the kingdom of Bagumi—the first step in his plan to destroy the man he should have called father. *King Ibrahim Aziz Saene.*

Soft footsteps behind reminded him he wasn't alone. The Zanzibar Convention Centre brimmed with thousands of guests attending the annual Children's Foundation Gala, one of the biggest charity events in Africa. Tickets were pegged at a thousand US dollars each, with the proceeds going to several charities across the continent. Like most such events, however, many attendees used it for networking, some to brag about their altruistic deeds, and others for the opportunity to rub shoulders with the rich and mighty.

Normally, he avoided such pomp and pageantry. The way he saw it, there had to be something fundamentally wrong with making a big show of one's good deeds. He preferred to make anonymous donations to many of the causes he supported. He'd broken protocol this time for one reason only:

To observe the enemy.

As luck would have it, King Ibrahim was the guest of honour this year, a privilege which came with the price tag of a hefty 'donation'—a gimmick undoubtedly meant to garner some international media attention. An hour into the event, neither the king nor a representative had made an appearance. His absence hadn't slowed down the festivities, though.

Finding the glitz and glamour strenuous, Kal had stolen out of the massive ballroom and taken refuge on one of several balconies. As it turned out, his escape from the flashlights and idle conversation hadn't gone unnoticed.

He gritted his teeth, bringing his mind back to the present and the person who'd interrupted his solitude. The last thing he needed was the company of a stargazing woman who'd spent a thousand dollars in hopes of catching the eye of a prince. Someone ought to save her from herself and rip the plaster off that fantasy. He was as good a candidate as any. After all, he might be the son of a king, but he wasn't Prince Charming. The sooner he made that clear and got rid of her, the better.

"What makes you think I'm not royalty?" He turned, lips pursed to dish out some tough love, yet the words didn't form.

He found himself entranced by the way the lights from the ballroom played against every rounded curve, awakening something primitive in him. She looked to be about five-foot-six, discounting the extra height afforded by her shoes. Her face remained shrouded in the dimness of the balcony.

Intrigued, he knew he'd pay any price to find out what she looked like. She stepped forward, and suddenly, her face was bathed in a beam of light slicing through the darkness from ... he didn't care to check where.

She held him captive with the most exquisite eyes he'd ever seen. An intense brown, like smoked honey, with a sparkle of gold in the left one where the light reflected off it. Their radiance would have laid his soul bare if he hadn't been standing in the shadows. With her entire face concealed behind an elaborate tattoo of ethnic make-up designed to give the appearance of a veil, she was mystery personified. She made easy prey of him as desire flared in his being with a fierceness that challenged reason.

Her effect didn't end at the physical, though. It ran deeper, reached him on an instinctive and spiritual level. *Like a soul mate.*

He shook away the errant thought, hoping she hadn't sensed his momentary confusion.

"For one," she started, "you're hiding out here instead of basking in the limelight."

He quirked a brow. *Hiding?*

Her lush lips curved up, revealing an even row of pearly whites invoking a vision of her nibbling on his earlobe. Somehow, he knew her teeth on his skin would be—

He snapped out of the reverie, forcing his mind to focus. Clearly, his unintended celibacy—the result of focusing too intently on revenge—needed to be rectified. How long had it been? Six months? More?

She mocked him with a chuckle. "I saw you inside. You were the picture of boredom."

Now he realised it wasn't her first remark that had snagged his attention, but rather her voice. It had an ethereal quality that seeped through him and did the impossible. He'd always felt restless, had often grappled with a compulsion to move, to do, to be on alert. When she'd spoken, the ever-present static in his mind had quietened. Her voice had stilled the storm within him. The sudden calm slammed into him with such force, he nearly doubled over at the impact.

By God. What was this?

He took in a deep breath, quelling the mêlée of shock and euphoria, told himself this couldn't possibly be real. Perhaps his thoughts of vengeance had tripped his senses, lured him into a trap of his own emotions. He never relied on sentiment to make decisions in any facet of his life—especially when it came to bedding a woman.

Whoa! When did he decide he was going to sleep with her?

He ignored the taunt, having no time for misgivings. He never hesitated when going for something he wanted, be it a company or a woman.

She hadn't taken another step forward, as if intentionally putting herself on display for his pleasure. His gaze snagged on her elaborate 'veil.' Masks were popular at the gala. She hadn't gone for the norm, though, something she could simply take off. The tribal undertones made it even more arresting, made her more captivating. A jewel hiding in plain sight.

Who was this vision in a piece of elegance and with the delicately cupped breasts that would fit perfectly in his hands? His eyes narrowed, lingering. *No.* They'd spill over just enough to entice his lips to them. Her waist, covered entirely with layers of stringed gemstones, tempted him to glide his hand over them. Would she feel the warmth of his touch?

He balled his hands into fists of resistance.

While he enjoyed the visual excursion she presented, he'd much rather she were displayed for his viewing in full naked glory, so he could adore her curves as they were clearly meant to be. What would she do if he held her? What if, emboldened, he pulled her forward, captured her full lower lip in his teeth, and nibbled? Would she offer him her tongue? Wrap her arms around him? Invite him to discover the treasures concealed beneath her clothes?

Merde! He reminded himself of the futility of his imaginings. Her first statement had made it clear she sought a prince. Bile rose up his throat—a testament to the extent of his distaste for the notion.

"I'm not a prince, and I don't desire to be one. You might want to move along."

She raised a hand and fluttered her fingers in a queenlike fashion. The title of queen would certainly suit her. She possessed the looks, the grace and … that extra something many women searched for but most never found.

"If I were looking for a prince, I'd be inside," she said. "I came out here to find you."

A giddy sensation exploded within him, chasing away the darkness engulfing him at the idea of her and Prince Charming together. However, a sliver of suspicion rooted him to the ground.

As a man on a mission that could bring down an entire nation, he couldn't take anything for granted. He'd been discreet in his reconnaissance of King Ibrahim and the Kingdom of Bagumi. As a successful financier specialising in corporate takeovers, discretion counted for everything. He'd taken all necessary precautions, but now, he wondered if he'd allowed his hatred for the man to affect his focus. Had he failed to cover his tracks as well as he'd thought?

He needed to distract her. Experience told him of one sure way to achieve it. Seduction.

He stepped out of the shadows, stopping close enough that he could reach out and touch her. Satisfaction brewed and swelled as he noted her sharp intake of breath.

"You look far too innocent to utter such words."

Her gaze dropped, colliding with his chest. Her lips parted as her focus hastened back up. Instead of the apprehension he'd expected, desire stared back at him. His pulse responded with exuberance. For the first time tonight, he began to see the bare-chested warrior costume his stylist had foisted on him as a plus.

She blinked, visibly regaining composure. "I didn't know innocence could be judged by sight."

Sassy. He'd give her that.

"There's a lot I can discern at a glance."

"You sound confident."

"I have no reason not to be."

"Maybe innocence is part of my act."

He searched her eyes. They were open, guileless—like someone who had nothing to hide.

He shook his head in absolute conviction. "Except it's not. I see it in your face, your expression ... your persona. You couldn't fake it if you wanted to."

The moment he finished speaking, the desire which had been receding surged back into her eyes and socked him in the chest. It revealed exactly what context she'd taken his words. In seconds, his mind went right there with her.

"Would it bother you?" she asked in a soft, almost hesitant voice.

"Innocence is a quality easily affected by many women." He paused, unable to prevent his gaze from roving over her as less-than-virtuous thoughts saturated his mind. "The true kind is refreshing."

"Now I'm sure you're no prince. Their education doesn't include flattery."

He caught a whiff of her scent—something wild yet feminine. It taunted every masculine cell in his body, but he didn't want to scare her with his considerably bigger stature. He held her gaze.

"I don't flatter, Honey Eyes. I may flirt with danger occasionally, tempt fate even, but flattery isn't in my nature."

"Danger?" She laughed, an incredibly beautiful sound, ensnaring him like a siren's song. "Do I look dangerous?"

"Said the splinter to the lion. I'd tread carefully if I were you."

"If I'm the splinter, then perhaps it's you who should be careful."

He allowed a smile. "I consider myself forewarned."

Their gazes locked. Heat flared between them. This time when she blinked, she couldn't sweep away her desire. Flirting had brought them to a crossroads. Turn right to keep going; left to retreat. He waited for her to make the call, half-expecting her to take Door Number Two—seek refuge in more innocent banter or invent an excuse to return to the party. Safety in numbers and all.

"I've been treading carefully my whole life," she surprised him by saying. "Tonight, I walk on the wild side."

He laughed softly. Maybe not so innocent, after all.

"The wild side, hm? I can take you there, my splinter, if that's what you want."

By now, he was certain she had no link to King Ibrahim. His intelligence team would already have alerted him. If word had somehow reached the king of Bagumi about Kal's investigations, it would seem he'd picked the one person alive who could momentarily shift his focus.

"Take me there, Warrior." Her sweet command, though whispered, drowned out every other sound.

He extended a hand. "Come."

She stared at his proffered invitation, indecision warring with desire in her eyes. Their relative sizes occurred to him anew. At six-three, he towered over her by nearly a foot. His muscular build and warrior costume—though overly embellished—probably didn't help. The arm guard with metallic tentacles snaking up to form a cuff around his biceps, already a snug fit, suddenly seemed to be cutting off his blood supply. A faux leopard skin cape draped over his other arm provided the only covering for his upper body. Even the *shendyt* covering his loins didn't make him look any less ... manly, as his brother had put it.

Then again, she'd been the one to encroach on his privacy. She didn't get to look at him as if he were a menace. He posed no threat. Unless she turned out to have an agenda. In which case, she—and whoever had sent her—would discover the most dangerous predators struck without warning and inflicted deadly bites.

He vacated the thought, preferring to return to the exhilaration of bantering with her.

"You hesitate."

She snapped her head up, her eyes colliding with his. For the briefest of seconds, he witnessed a depth of desire he hadn't expected without having even touched her yet. He saw something else. Lust. Pure and unbridled, as if it had been brewed in the cauldrons of Eros.

"It isn't hesitation if I already know what I want."

She placed her hand in his. The contact, a spark of electricity, compelled his fingers to close around her hand instead of the instinct to pull away as if from danger. Yielding to the force which had led them to this point, he tugged her into his arms, draping her left arm over his shoulder.

As her supple curves melded against him, she tilted her head fully in a natural motion to meet his gaze. Her lips parted as though she'd resorted to breathing out of her mouth. They beckoned, but he resisted the urge to dip his head for a taste, knowing the build-up of anticipation would make the eventual surrender more satisfying. If it didn't kill him first.

"Dance with me," he said.

He swayed her sideways, the beginning of a waltz. The crystal beads surrounding her waist rubbed against his lower abdomen, causing erotic friction. If he didn't start a conversation to get his mind off how good it felt, he'd be hoisting her on his shoulder and hauling her off to the nearest bed.

"What do I call you?" he asked.

"No names," she whispered in a tone laced with urgency.

He raised a brow, curiosity aroused, then tempered it down, deciding against probing.

"Too bad. My name would sound beautiful on your lips."

No matter how much she affected him, this would unfortunately be a one-time deal. After tonight, he'd be embarking on a dangerous mission, one which couldn't accommodate the entanglements of a woman awaiting his return.

Yet, it didn't keep him from wondering at her reasons for wanting to hide her identity. Who was this woman, and why did he want to unravel her secrets?

CHAPTER TWO

Princess Edina Dampare blinked, expecting to awaken any moment, because this had to be a dream. She didn't flirt or tease let alone pursue men onto secluded balconies and practically proposition them. Not even ones who looked like they were sired from the loins of gods.

He met her gaze, and she noted the light of intrigue in his eyes, expected him to press for a name. His words echoed in her mind.

"My name would sound beautiful on your lips."

He'd spoken in the manner of a man who knew his way about a woman's body. His sexy, self-assured voice evoked imaginings of being slowly undressed by him, of crying out his name even though she had no idea what it was.

Inside, she trembled. Not from fear—at least not a fear of him, but of her decision to pursue him, of the extent of his effect on her, of how quickly he'd spotted her lack of experience, of being rejected by this stranger.

She straightened her posture although she knew from years of comportment lessons that she hadn't been slouching. Hopefully, his skills of discernment didn't include mind-reading.

"You're not very modest, are you?" she said.

"Modesty has its place. Pretence is a wasted effort I don't indulge in."

She chuckled, though his lack of a smile indicated he hadn't meant it as a joke. "Your sense of self-worth is astounding."

He pulled back. For a second, she worried she might have offended him, but then realised he was setting the stage for a full body turn. On cue, she released his shoulder, swishing her now free left hand in a stylish movement while executing the move. She swayed her hips a little more—because, of course, he was going to watch her ass—before returning to her original position against the solid wall of his chest. She'd had many occasions to be grateful for the dance lessons she'd had to take as a little girl, but never as much as she did now, witnessing the appreciation in his eyes.

Her mind drifted back to her first dance lesson at age four. All her protests had bounced off her mother's insistence that 'a princess should know how to dance' as though it were a written law. She'd grown up with a long list of things a princess had to do regardless of her desire to do them.

She brought her mind back to the present, noted his fluid movements.

"You must have taken dance lessons growing up."

"Suffered through them would be more accurate." His lips curled up in a smile. "My mother was determined to raise me into a gentleman."

"From what I see, she succeeded."

His easy acceptance of her wish for anonymity had been testament enough, but more than that, he exuded a self-assuredness that would put most men to shame. He carried his sense of entitlement with a level of finesse befitting a king. Yet, she sensed he might consider this an insult.

"Can I ask you a question?"

"Ask me anything."

His voice had a natural gravelly quality that made her want to close her eyes and absorb it.

"Do you have something against people of royal birth?" At his raised eyebrows, and because she didn't want to give him a chance to deflect, she added, "Most people are flattered to be associated with royalty, but you seemed offended by my earlier remark."

He stiffened so slightly, she'd have missed it if their bodies weren't touching.

"Would it be so bad if you were a prince?"

"I don't see royal birth as an achievement." His tone was disdain and little else.

"Perhaps not, but most people would tell you being royal is a big deal. Opens doors which would, otherwise, be closed to you."

"I'm not most people, Honey Eyes."

The deep timbre of his voice went straight from her ears to her core, and her inner muscles did a tighten-and-release dance.

"I'm naturally opposed to the idea of handing supreme power to anyone simply because of the blood running through their veins. History has proven too many times that kings usurp their powers. They manipulate their subjects and look down on anyone they deem beneath their station."

She gave a gentle snort of understanding. What would he think of the events taking place in her country, the kingdom of Umaasie? Her brother, the current ruler, sought to broker a marriage alliance between her and a yet unnamed suitor. It was precisely why she'd needed to do this. She wanted to experience the kind of passion a woman shared with a man before signing her life over to a loveless, passionless marriage meant to advance the kingdom's political and economic future.

She shook her head, bringing her mind back to the present, to the one who called her *Honey Eyes*. His expression remained schooled, but the spite in his words hadn't gone unnoticed. It alluded to personal undertones. What was his story? Had he, or someone he knew, been mistreated by a royal? Did she want to know?

No, she decided, not wanting to mar her evening. Tonight was hers; nothing else mattered.

They moved in silence, communicating only through body language, each pivot and turn flowing gracefully into the next, every touch of their bodies heating her blood, fuelling the electricity crackling between them, heightening her desire. Under the scrutiny of his dark, intense stare, awareness sizzled. Heat swirled in her lower belly, resulting in an ache farther down.

The sound of clapping drifted over, snapping her out of the delicious thoughts and reminding her they were in a public place—albeit currently alone. The music had ended. Disappointed, she began to withdraw, but he held her in place, resuming their dance.

"The song——" she started to say.

"Music isn't confined to what the ears hear," he whispered.

From any other pair of lips, it would have been downright corny. From him, nothing had sounded more romantic.

"Not just a handsome face. A dancer *and* a poet." She fell back into step, expecting awkwardness at dancing to no music. To her surprise, she felt no discomfiture as they moved in perfect unison.

He smiled without commenting. Relaxing further, she leant in. The lack of music heightened her consciousness of him, the smoothness of his skin beneath her hands, and of herself, heart beating an unfamiliar rhythm. The silence magnified the sounds of the night as though nature itself had determined to grace them with its song. Now, the only unnatural thing was the idea of leaving his arms.

"Your turn to answer a question." He led her in a pivot, and then a dip. He paused with her back arched over his arm, forcing her to grip his shoulder for support. "What do you do? Or is it off-topic, too?"

She swallowed, rendered temporarily speechless as his dark eyes bore into hers with intensity. He straightened them back, seemingly oblivious to the momentary scrambling of her brain caused by his closeness.

"Curator," she replied, glad to note her voice came out steady. Thankfully, with a degree in archaeology and museum studies, she'd fitted right in at the Royal Museum of Umaasie, which provided an easy cover whenever she needed it. Like right now. "Boring, I know."

"*Au contraire*," he said in a West African French accent. "Custodian of historical heritage. You should be admired and feared at the same time."

"Twice tonight, you've called me dangerous. I should be offended." Despite her words, her heart skipped a beat, tempering into a giddy tempo before settling into a rhythm slightly more buoyant than usual.

"Yet, your beautiful eyes betray your delight."

She couldn't help smiling. "What about you?"

"I'm an investor."

"In what?"

"Let's just say I'm a jack of all trades. I have a knack for identifying lucrative ventures." A beat passed. "Do you work in a museum or a gallery?"

His voice resonated with a timbre of intimacy as if he'd asked something much more personal. Captivated in its allure, it took her a moment to refocus her mind on his question. Still, she gave him a look to tell him his smooth change of subject hadn't gone unnoticed.

"Wait. Let me hazard a guess," he said before she'd decided whether to swerve the query. He squinted as if in deep thought. "Museum."

She stiffened. Apprehension seeped into her veins. Had her brother discovered her plan? Had he sent this man to entice her just to send her back home?

Can't be. She forced herself to keep her mind rational. Her brother didn't do subtle. If he'd caught wind of what she plotted to do tonight, the Royal Guard of Umaasie would have been sent to marshal her back to her country to face the music.

The thought calmed her heart, but not her curiosity. "Are you sure we haven't met before?"

It would make sense—the strong attraction and easy verbal exchange. As a princess of Umaasie, and head curator of the royal museum, meet-and-greets were a frequent occurrence. It stood to reason she wouldn't remember every single acquaintance.

"You think it's possible we're previously acquainted and neither of us remembers?"

"No, you're right," she admitted.

No way would she be able to forget if she'd laid eyes on him before. It wasn't just about his looks. This man had something more, something she couldn't pinpoint exactly, but knew she was on the verge of succumbing to it.

"What made you choose museum? Don't you think I have what it takes to handle the glamour of art?"

"I think a museum matches your personality more."

"We've never met, and yet, you purport to know my nature?"

His answering smile put flutters in her stomach.

"I have an instinct when it comes to reading people, and it's never steered me wrong."

"What does your intuition say about me?"

"You're dressed like a goddess, but you've hidden your face. It tells me you know your worth, but you're not out to flaunt your beauty. You could have worn a mask, but you chose to paint a design instead. While you may be subtle about it, you like to stand apart. Undoubtedly, only the right eyes will recognise your true value. You followed me out here in defiance of any social dictates of what's proper or improper for a woman to do, which suggests you're not afraid to challenge convention."

She swallowed down the impulse to confess the real reason for her disguise. She couldn't exactly tell a man to whom she hoped to lose her virginity that she'd soon be married—it could be in a couple of months or a year, but it was a certainty. She definitely couldn't confess he was her last-ditch act of defiance against a royal decree that dictated the terms of her marriage.

"My instinct tells me tonight won't easily be forgotten," he said.

Her gaze dropped to his lips, and suddenly, all she could think of was how much she wanted him to kiss her. Maybe if it led to more, she'd hear him whisper those things in a voice that would make her orgasm so fast and hard, she'd reel.

Whoa! Where had that come from? She'd never wanted a man with such force that it overloaded her brain with thoughts of sex. She trembled with the magnitude of her desire, terrified yet emboldened. If she didn't exercise caution, she'd be begging him to make love to her right here. She had to calm down if only to ensure she didn't fumble her way through the experience like a high school girl with a crush.

"I thought you didn't flatter, Warrior."

He chuckled. "Truth should never be mistaken for flattery."

"Do you always speak the truth?" she found herself asking, not sure why it even mattered since she'd lied to him by omission about her identity.

"My word is my bond, Honey Eyes. You'll only hear truth from my lips."

The dance had slowed down, she realised. They now swayed from side to side in one spot. Her arm had found a comfortable place wrapped around his nape while his hands rested on the small of her back. Parts of her she'd always known existed now announced their presence with heat and insistent quivers. His lips, like a magnet, reeled her in with each breath she exhaled until they were mere inches away, his gaze never breaking connection.

"What else do your lips do?"

Warmth blazed her face as she realised she'd said it out loud. Her shame notwithstanding, she couldn't help staring at his mouth. She wasn't into extremes when it came to lip size—not too thick, and definitely not too thin. This African warrior had a perfect set. Lush, a tad too full on a man, with the most sinful pout. They looked like they'd be soft yet firm and oh-so-kissable.

Stop staring. The caution proved pointless. She must have looked long enough for him to notice, because he stopped moving completely and pulled her closer.

"This," he whispered, as the space between them began to shrink.

Her eyes closed, and her lips parted. Her heart hammered against her ribcage in expectation. For several beats, he didn't kiss her, and she began to wonder if she'd jumped the gun. Then she heard it.

Ten, nine, eight …

The countdown to the New Year.

Seven, six, five …

She felt it. His warm breath like a gentle breeze fanning her face.

Four, three, two …

His hand glided up from her waist, its effect like a flame scorching her skin.

One!

"Happy New Year, Goddess."

His lips brushed against hers. She didn't hesitate in opening up to him.

There was nothing tentative about his kiss, no testing the waters. He tipped her head back and took possession of her mouth as if she were his for the taking. The contact packed the force of a mini-explosive.

The instant their tongues touched, a moan flared out of her. In response, he delved deeper, his warm tongue teasing and probing, executing deliberate strokes of bliss, until she stopped thinking altogether and only felt.

When he pulled back, she couldn't turn away from his fiery gaze. The rest of the world fell away, leaving just the two of them—suspended in time. Something shifted within her and hooked onto him, connecting them. Her heart lurched, sick with the realisation she'd never see him again after tonight. Did he feel the same? What if she told him the truth?

She dismissed the inane idea instantly. Even if he proved worthy of such trust, what authority did he have to prevent the inevitable?

As for her, she might have no power to decide who she married, but she refused to relinquish her right to choose who she gave her body to for the first time. And she picked him.

CHAPTER THREE

Kalahari had thought he'd be stronger than his desire, that one kiss would satisfy him, strengthen his resolve enough to send her on her way and focus on his mission.

He'd been wrong.

As she hung on to him, puckered lips slightly parted in a blatant desire for more, he admitted what he should have known from the start. One kiss with this woman, no matter how explosive, would never suffice.

Feeling her soft lips, tasting the warmth of her tongue, had unleashed a desire so strong that he barely managed to hang on to the reins of restraint.

"You have talented lips."

Her breathy remark whispered deliciously against his mouth.

It was probably pig-headed of him to be pleased about her compliment, but he couldn't help the satisfaction burgeoning within him. He wanted to touch her, kiss her, hear her sounds of pleasure as they surged to a higher level of intimacy.

"There's more to me than talented lips."

"Show me."

Her audacious request equally matched his own yearning for more.

Despite her face being mere breaths away, he cupped her chin, angled her head a fraction before capturing her soft, full lips again.

He'd delved into the first kiss, jumped in headfirst and taken possession of her mouth. This time, he took it slow, savouring her lower lip and allowing her to set the pace. She responded by treating his upper lip to delectable nibbles and tugs. With intertwined fingers, she wrapped her hands around his nape, forcing him to lean further down.

Her tongue came out to play, warm, velvety, and yielding, tasting of champagne and mint. Blood rushed down to the part of him that hardened at the idea of also feeling her warm tongue. She pressed into him, rubbing against his growing arousal. The gesture knocked his resolve down a few more notches. He grunted, holding on, determined to let her lead.

She pulled back and thrust her pelvis forward again. "Touch me there."

The boldness surprised him, pleased him. She wanted him as much as he did her. The crystal beads covering her abdomen rubbed against his hardness through the fabric of his loin cloth. Shards of pleasure-pain spiked through him, dashing his remaining resolve to smithereens.

He swore, trailing his hand down her waist to cup her ass. "Jump."

She leapt in sync with his move to lift her, locking strong thighs around him. He whipped her around, leaning her against a pillar. As the kiss deepened, one hand held her firm while the other journeyed down the curve of her butt, seeking her centre. His fingertips encountered damp panties.

By God! He hardened further.

He'd have liked to tease, bring her to the point of pleading before breaching the constraints of the delicate fabric. He was too far gone in his desire, however. He wanted her wetness around his fingers too much to wait. Plus, she'd already issued a command. He swept aside the seat of her panties, found her hot and slick. With a grunt, he slipped his finger inside her heat.

She gasped in a breath, tightening her thighs around his waist.

"Goddess," he groaned. "You're already so wet."

She made a sound between a moan and a whimper and pumped her hips. He didn't need any further encouragement to move his finger in rhythm with her thrusts. He wanted more. By God, he wanted to get rid of all these clothes and sink so deep inside her he'd lose himself. He pulled out, brought his slick finger to her clit, and rubbed gently. She cried out, breaking the kiss as she tossed her head back.

"You like this," he whispered. A statement rather than a question.

"Mm-hm," she moaned her response anyway. "Don't stop."

He obliged, alternating between her clit and her core. Her inner muscles started to clench around his fingers as she began to climax. He kissed her, absorbing the scream ripping out of her. She might be feeling wild tonight, but he sensed she wouldn't want to attract an audience. Neither would he.

He continued to hold her several moments after she'd stopped trembling from her release. Finally, he eased her back to her feet. She clung to him, and he knew the exact moment she became aware of his throbbing erection. She stilled, sucked in a breath, then pumped her hips forward as if ensuring it was truly there.

"You're hard."

Despite himself, he laughed. A harsh, guttural sound he almost didn't recognise.

"Honey Eyes, I'll need all night to get rid of that."

"I have tonight."

Her combined look of desire, determination, and wonder made him want to heft her onto the balustrade and take her right there and then. If he'd had protection, he might have thrown caution to the wind and done exactly that, but his blasted *shendyt* didn't come with pockets.

"Not here."

After the words came out, he realised their implication—abandoning his mission.

Only for tonight.

He tried to take a mental step back, remind himself of the reasons he'd set out to pursue King Ibrahim in the first place.

She moved, creating space to slip her hand between them. She touched him, the contact slight, barely there, but its impact all-encompassing nevertheless. Blood rushed from his brain, compelled all his mental faculties to converge on her, abandoning thoughts of vengeance.

"Let's get out of here."

***

Edina half-expected her conviction to waiver when they stepped into the demure lighting in the foyer. Glancing over at him, however, she realised the magic wasn't confined to the balcony and its bewitching shadows. His effect seemed even more potent with the benefit of light. Her legs jellified under the weight of her desire.

To their right, a closed door led back to the banquet hall, where the gala continued in full swing. He led her the other way, towards the elevators, and she followed on autopilot, her heart pounding in anticipation.

While waiting for the elevator to reach their floor, he faced her.

"Give me your mobile."

She frowned, but fished the phone from her clutch purse, entered her four-digit code to access the home screen, and handed it over.

After a couple of taps, he held up the phone and snapped a selfie. She raised her brows, meaning to comment about the demerits of vanity.

"You're safe with me, but to remove any doubt from your mind, you have my photo," he said. "You can send it to someone you trust. Though I'd entreat you to delete it after tonight."

As she took back the device, their fingers brushed. The touch was electric—just like before— causing her heart to flutter. She held her breath for a moment in a bid to calm her racing pulse.

How many men would go the extra mile to assure her of her safety even when it had been the farthest thing from her mind? It said one thing: he may not be Prince Charming as he put it, but this was a man apart—a man she might have wished to know if she weren't fated for a political marriage. She considered sending the photo to her best friend, Jamila, who at this very moment sat at the table reserved for Princess Edina.

She quickly discarded the idea. Jamila had already risked a lot by impersonating a princess. She wouldn't want to further impose even though her best friend would never complain. Besides, Edina couldn't risk her message being intercepted, especially by her brother. When she'd set out to defy him this way, she'd known what she was getting herself into.

The warrior was a big man. If his corded arms were any indication, he had matching strength. During her combat lessons, she particularly excelled at using bigger opponents' strength against them. One-on-one, she could hold her own.

She slipped the phone back into her purse. "Thank you, but I'm not in doubt."

Her response pleased him, judging from the small smile touching the corners of his lips. Amazing that it somehow made it to his eyes. The elevator dinged at that moment.

***

Much later, they stepped out of another elevator and into a small lobby, facing the penthouse suite of a plush boutique hotel that catered to a *crème de la crème* clientèle. They knew how to be discrete—according to Jamila who'd raved about it on her visit to Zanzibar a year ago.

He'd let her pick the place; she supposed another of his several gestures to assure her she was in control of what happened tonight. However, he'd called in advance to make the reservation, which suited her fine since he had more experience in ... well, liaisons.

He swiped the card and opened the door, stepping aside to give her way.

Her heart pounded, the enormity of the moment dawning. Once she entered, there'd be no turning back. Her actions tonight could have implications not just for her, but for her country as well. The same country, she reminded herself, which had dictated her actions from the day she was born, and now demanded her marriage be for its benefit rather than hers. Did she not deserve one night of selfishness before imprisoning her heart forever?

She stepped in, abandoning all thoughts of her title and its obligations as the door clicked shut.

"Can I offer you a drink?" he asked.

She wanted to remind him this wasn't his hotel room, but somehow, she knew he'd have arranged for a full bar. However, she didn't desire liquid confidence for tonight. She'd reserve that for her wedding night. With him, she wanted to feel every sensation, needed to embrace her emotions and own each of her actions.

She shook her head. "I only want you."

A fierce passion sharpened his gaze. He released a sound that was part groan, part growl. Instead of pouncing as she expected—hoped?—he began undressing. The animal skin cape draped over his shoulder came off first, revealing the expanse of his chest. Her gaze drank in the perfection of his bare torso. The bunching of muscles, as he placed the garment on the coat stand, drew her attention to his broad shoulders. Her pulse escalated.

His neck and arm ornaments also found a spot on the stand. His headgear followed, exposing hair about two inches long on top and shorter on the sides, complemented by his chin-strap beard and goatee. She sucked in a breath, unashamedly taking him in. Handsome didn't begin to cover the magnificence of his maleness. A sculpted build like his could only be honed through unrelenting discipline—a testament to the intangible essence of him. He put her senses on overdrive, made her quiver and want.

He closed the space between them in two strides.

This is it. Anticipation heightened her need, overpowering any inherent nerves. He reached for the beaded strap of her gown, the tips of his fingers grazing her skin, sparking flames of desire. She held her breath.

"Stunning outfit. We wouldn't want to ruin it."

She smiled. "Thank you for caring about the fate of my dress."

"I was raised by a fashion designer." He frowned as if he'd confessed more information than intended. "I've learnt carelessness with clothes is a cardinal sin."

His confession revealed little, and yet, she found herself filing away that scrap of insight for later musings. Right now, she focused on him moving around to her back. As he drew down the zip tab, the garment released its hold. He then eased the straps off her shoulders, and the dress, aided by the gemstone detail around her waist, fell in a heap at her feet. Wearing no bra, she stood in nothing but her jewellery and lace panties. With her back facing him, she was left wondering what he'd do next.

She didn't have to wait long to find out as he swept aside her twist braids and kissed the nape of her neck. A soft moan sounded in her throat. How come she'd never known how sensitive that part of her could be? As he continued his kiss along her shoulder, one of his hands slipped around to her belly, pulling her into him until she felt the hard evidence of his desire settled against her.

Her own need intensified, and she whipped around, seeking his mouth. As though expecting it, he met her halfway, joining their lips. She wrapped her arms around him, exploring the muscular slopes of his shoulders and back. He lifted her without breaking the kiss, the sensation of being air-borne only adding to the giddy sensation. Moments later, he laid her on a king-sized bed, his lips grazing her neck as he pulled away. She angled her head to give him room, wanting more, needing more of him. At her invitation, he released a deep groan and nibbled. Her breathing accelerated under the feel of his lips and tongue, and even teeth, leaving a love bite on her skin.

Moving from her neck that still smarted from his ministrations, he trailed his tongue down to her breast. The beaded peak craved his attention. She arched up, proffering a bold invitation. He took her nipple in, sucking and nipping, extracting a deep moan from her. He paid similar attention to her other breast, alternating between the two in a practiced rhythm that pushed her towards a state of mindlessness.

"Oh," she cried, writhing beneath him.

He continued his sweet torture, teasing out her pleasure spots with every caress, bite, lick, and kiss. By the time he reached the V at the apex of her thighs, she could no longer control the chorus of pleasured sounds flowing from her mouth. His own breaths had become more laboured, giving way to an impatient groan just before he slipped his fingers between her and the lace panties she still wore. His trim nails grazed her sensitised skin as he tugged the flimsy undergarment down her trembling limbs. Her breath shortened from expectancy as he parted her legs, exposing her most intimate place to his view.

He'd already touched her there, felt her come around his fingers. Yet, watching him look seemed more intimate somehow. A wave of vulnerability swept through her, but the anticipated attack of self-consciousness didn't materialise. His ravenous and appreciative gaze left no room for inhibitions.

"You're gorgeous," he murmured with a look of awe.

When he buried his head between her thighs and released a hungry groan, she felt like the goddess he'd called her—powerful and in control even as she succumbed to his mastery. His fingers parted her folds, opening her further to take his first taste of her. His warm tongue circled around her slick, sensitive bud before he closed his mouth over it and sucked. A cry erupted from her lips.

"You taste so good, Goddess," he grunted.

Her moans rose uncurbed as she writhed from the overpowering sensations. With both hands at her hips, he constrained her movements as he nipped, pressed, and tugged, forcing her to feel the impact of every nibble, every lick, every suck …

After her first release at the ministrations of his hands, she'd thought that had been it for her, and the rest of the night would be for his pleasure. She'd been wrong. Amidst her cries of rapture, she began to climax. It started as a warm sensation and burgeoned into something molten, taking over her entire being. His delicious assault continued, unyielding, pushing her forward until she teetered at the edge.

He hummed, the sound of pure gratification, which vibrated in her centre before cascading through the rest of her. It proved to be the final push to hurl her into a blissful free fall even more intense than her first. She grabbed his hands and held on.

It wasn't until the tremors had subsided and her breathing had come under reasonable control that she released her iron grip on his fingers.

When he met her gaze, his eyes held tenderness that shouldn't be possible. They'd met only a few hours ago. There should be no emotions between them. Yet, he felt familiar to her heart—as if she'd known him in another lifetime—and his expression told her he felt the same.

"I can't wait to be inside you."

His words put delicious flutters in her belly. Was every man this attentive?

"Me neither."

He got up from the bed, leaving her yearning for his warmth, his touch. She wanted to admonish him for his abandonment, but her mind preferred to focus on watching him. Her gaze went to the *shendyt* now forming an impressive tent over his arousal. He unclipped the waistband and let the garment fall, exposing the black briefs underneath. Those came off, too, and then he stood before her, spellbinding in his virility. At the sight of his erection, her need intensified.

He climbed back onto the bed while ripping open a packet of protection. It seemed the most natural thing to part her legs in readiness for him.

"Wait." The word tumbled out of her mouth, as she sat up. "Let me feel you."

He halted his movement. Her hands encircled him, and she heard him inhale sharply. He was warm and smooth and rigid. She moved her palm along the length of him, relishing her effect on him as he grew bigger and harder in her grip.

His body trembled.

"Goddess," he muttered on a harsh breath.

Desire inflamed, she moved her hand in the opposite direction, ending at his rounded tip, and pumped a few times. He cursed, and suddenly pulled out of her grasp. The flame of lust burning in his eyes assuaged any concerns she'd done something wrong.

"I don't want to come in your hand, *Chérie.*"

She nodded. Without further words, he sheathed himself. She laid back as he rose over her, nestling his engorged tip at her opening. Meeting her gaze again, he began his entry. She didn't look away, needing him to know they were taking this step together.

He met her body's resistance, and she gasped. He stilled, and for several moments stared into her eyes, his surprise evident. Alarm shot through her. He wouldn't change his mind now, would he? It took a few seconds for her to realise he hadn't retreated.

It hit her then. He sought her permission.

She returned his stare in wonderment of his sense of honour. Even now when he'd all but claimed her, he'd stop if she asked? It proved she'd chosen right. She didn't want him to stop. She wanted it, needed it ... needed *him*.

"Yes," she whispered, clamping down on a wish that this wouldn't be a one-time affair.

Despite her assent, he began to pull out. In reflex, she grabbed his ass, keeping him connected to her.

His lips curved into a toe-curling half-smile. "Patience, Honey Eyes."

"I don't want you to stop."

"I'm not."

For a moment, he continued to stare into her eyes, not moving as if demanding her complete trust. When she'd given it in a nod, he slipped his hand around her thigh, lifting her leg, opening her up before resuming his entry. She trembled, her heart expanding as he filled her.

His moan of satisfaction echoed hers. He repeated the motion, sinking further each time, letting her sheath learn on its own how to adjust to his girth until he'd coaxed her body into sweet submission. Her breath hitched as she tried to accommodate the myriad of sensations at being filled like this for the first time.

"Breathe," he whispered.

Her inhalation, a series of jagged puffs, turned into a gasp when he moved his hand to her breast and pinched her nipple. Immediately, he caressed, soothing the sting, introducing her to the exhilarating merger of pain and pleasure. She arched up, demanding more of it. He obliged while beginning to move inside her with deep, long, measured strokes.

The aching desire in her core surged. She matched his every thrust, her movements instinctive. Each time their bodies met, she shuddered, knowing she'd never be the same after tonight. She could've let the momentous discovery scare her. Instead, she chose to revel in the sensations flooding her body, bask in the feeling of completion she'd found with him. As they settled into a harmonious rhythm, her need escalated rapidly.

He continued to caress and tweak the hardened peaks of her breasts, creating waves of boundless delight ripping through her. He might as well have reached into her and touched her soul. It was too much and yet not nearly enough. So when he lowered his mouth to her ear and sucked on her earlobe, she angled her head, giving him full access.

"Oh, God," she cried out.

It was bliss, beyond her wildest imaginings; an onslaught of feelings she'd never experienced and didn't know how to control ... didn't *want* to control. She desired more of it, more of him. She wrapped her arms and legs around him, pulling him in, urging him to give her more.

Heeding her demands, he increased the pace, slamming into her. Fingers digging into his back, her impassioned cries mingled with his in rhythm with their sensual dance. It didn't take long before pressure began to build again, imploding without warning in pleasure more intense than anything she'd ever experienced. The force of it brought tears to her eyes.

Amidst her cries of ecstasy, she heard him let out a drawn-out groan, the tone rough and guttural. His body shook with his release, and then he stilled. She held him close, memorising the feel of his smooth, hard body. Tonight would live with her forever.

After a moment, his taut muscles began to relax. He pulled back, and for several seconds just stared into her eyes, their bodies still joined in the most intimate way.

"That was—you're ..." she began but realised she didn't yet have words to describe their exquisite union.

"No, Honey Eyes," he said, his voice raspy. "It's you."

"Is it always like this?" she asked, guessing the answer and yet hoping she was wrong.

He shook his head. "It's never been for me."

She breathed out. Sorrow washed over her as she let his words sink in. She'd never experience this feeling of euphoria again. Her eyes stung with the threat of tears. She blinked and looked away.

"Don't." His soft whisper was followed by a finger hooked under her chin, bringing her focus back to him. "We have all night, remember?"

Her lips quivered a bit while she moulded them into a smile. The thought of discovering more erotic pleasure at his hands eased the ache in her chest a bit. How was it possible to be joyous and sorrowful at the same time?

"That's better." After a moment, he finally pulled out. "Wait here."

A happy sigh left her lips as she admired his fine ass retreat into the bathroom. He emerged moments later with a towel. Before she could inquire what it was for, he began to clean her. A low moan rose from her when the warm cloth met her centre. Words locked in her throat at the reverence in his gaze and actions.

This man …

Neither of them spoke while he continued wiping her all over with ceremonial care. When he finished, he returned the towel to the bathroom. Back in bed, he stretched out beside her, propping himself on one elbow and staring down at her.

Unable to resist, she cupped his handsome face. The tips of her fingers dug into his hair, which despite the kinky surface, was softer than she'd expected. She trailed her hand downwards, teasing his beard. So many things went through her mind, each fighting for an audience. None could be spoken. She shouldn't be feeling anything substantial for this man. This stranger. And yet ...

His eyes narrowed. "What?"

Searching through her mind, she picked the least complicated of her musings. "I like your beard."

His brows edged upwards, as did the corners of his lips as if her comment left him both pleased and staggered. "Yeah?"

She nodded. "You look surprised."

"I've been told my hair and beard look scruffy."

She wriggled her nose in disagreement. The high top of loose dread-like twists of his hair softened his devastating handsomeness while lending a sexy bad-boy vibe to his gentility.

"Don't listen to them. Overly groomed beards with lined up edges look pretentious."

She made a show of shuddering at the idea. A low chuckle rumbled out of him, and his eyes sparkled. Seconds ticked by in silence, wherein she became aware of his intense scrutiny.

"What?" She mimicked his question.

"Why didn't you tell me?"

"Tell you what?"

"You hadn't been with a man before. I'd have taken my time."

His quiet confession had a thickening effect on the air around them. God, the way he spoke ... It was as if ... as if ...

No. She had to be reading more into his expression and tone than existed. To cover her own flush of emotions, she sought to lighten the moment.

Shrugging aside a bout of self-consciousness, she moulded her lips into what she hoped was a sexy, mysterious smile. "Guess your powers of discernment aren't as reliable as you claimed, Warrior."

He chuckled. As she'd hoped, some of the electricity crackling between them diffused.

"I stand corrected." He kissed her lightly. "Rest now, *ma chérie*. You'll need your stamina for the next round."

CHAPTER FOUR

Accra, Ghana - Present day

"Daydreaming again?"

Kal jerked his head up, swearing as his foster brother walked into his office. He didn't attempt to deny the accusation, but he sure as hell wasn't about to discuss it. Eight months. Over half a damn year, and he'd failed to get that night—to get *her*—out of his mind. Out of his system.

"Shaka, did no one teach you to knock before you enter?"

"What kind of brother would I be if I didn't catch you unawares once in a while?"

He grimaced.

Shaka grinned. "Besides, I did knock. You didn't answer."

He shook his head, returning his attention to his tablet. At nearly six p.m., the staff had already closed for the day. Precisely why he'd asked Shaka to come in at this time. He didn't need an audience for their discussion.

"I can find her, you know. If you'd let me," Shaka offered, as he'd done a few times before.

With a background in military special forces, Shaka's abilities in locating people who didn't want to be found were legendary. How, though, did they search for her when Kal had nothing but the image of a tattooed face etched in his mind? That and the memory of one explosive night which had both healed and scarred him.

She'd been adamant about them having just one night. He'd still been optimistic. In the pre-dawn hours when the time had come to say goodbye, he'd offered to drop her at her hotel. She'd insisted on a neutral venue where a vehicle had met them. Despite telling himself he didn't need the complications of a relationship, he'd realised he wanted to see her again. The feelings she aroused in him were too strong to ignore.

The need for more had compelled him to ask her name a second time. Her succulent lips had parted. Hope, as exhilarating as a drug, had charged his entire being. Then she'd brought him crashing down to Earth with her response. "*Honey Eyes. Just call me that.*" Never one to beg, he'd swallowed down his disappointment and bidden her goodbye.

He'd succumbed to his emotions and let down his guard, allowed her to affect him, to *infect* him with her essence. All efforts to eradicate her from his mind had proved futile.

He swore again.

"Hey, don't bite my head off." Shaka raised his hands in mock surrender as he sat. "Frankly, I'm surprised you had a one-night-stand on purpose. What's the thing you keep saying? Ah! If a woman's worth bedding, she's worth bedding more than once."

He offered a grunt in response. Growing up, with Mamaa as his only family, he'd yearned for connection. Her desire to give him what he'd wanted the most—a dad—had attracted one too many men intent on taking advantage of a woman they'd assumed to be helpless. He'd learnt valuable lessons witnessing her resilience. Lessons like not toying with women's emotions and never disregarding their wishes. If he did, then what would differentiate him from a man like King Ibrahim?

"She made her stance clear. I must respect it." His response burned through his throat on its way out. "Anyway, that's not what I need to focus on right now. The intel is confirmed. Prince Zawadi has announced his abdication."

Shaka's expression became serious. "You don't look surprised."

"I'm not. We both know what King Ibrahim is capable of. It doesn't take a stretch of the imagination to guess he'd screw his kid over to get his way. But I *am* impressed Zawadi chose his woman over the throne."

Shaka nodded. "I'd have bet on him putting up more of a fight for the throne. He's been groomed from birth for it."

"Someone should've taught him not to put all his eggs in one basket."

He didn't bother to mask his disdain. He didn't have to. Not with Shaka.

"I must admit, I feel a little sorry for the guy."

"Don't be," Kal said. "He's a tool."

"In his book, so are you."

He snorted, silently acknowledging the truth of it. Eight months ago, he'd been foolhardy. With his mother's passing so fresh on his heart, he hadn't fully thought his plan through. His rage had propelled him to attend the gala. He'd been eager to share the same space with King Ibrahim and shame him before the entire world with the truth of his existence.

He'd planned to capitalise on the media shitstorm bound to ensue and call in every favour to expose every bad deed the man had committed. No one could stand against the judgment of the global village the world had become—as many a world leader had discovered. By the end of it all, King Ibrahim would have had no option than to abdicate.

He'd been high on emotions. No wonder he'd so easily been swayed by a woman—but not just any woman. *Her.* Abandoning his mission that night had turned out to be a blessing in disguise. King Ibrahim had never made it to the banquet. He'd later discovered the reason.

After his third son, Prince Zediah, had rejected a marriage contract with the daughter of the president of neighbouring Barakat, the latter had taken offense. The resulting rise in tensions between the two countries had necessitated an emergency trip to smooth things over.

It had given Kal the opportunity to leash his anger, to focus it better. He'd expended his efforts towards becoming better versed in the politics of Bagumi and strategically insinuating himself into the economy. This had brought him into conflict with the Crown Prince on one occasion.

"So," Shaka said. "How do you exact revenge on a king in a nation where you have no official status?"

"I'll get an official status before going after what he holds dearest. His throne."

That's all he wanted—King Ibrahim's character sullied badly enough for his own people to reject him. As he'd done to Kal and his mother when he'd chosen his position and precious throne over them.

Shaka blinked. "Now I know you have a death wish. Short of creating a civil war, I don't see how you intend to accomplish your goal."

He gave in to a rare smile. "I have a plan."

Mamaa's, actually. Not that she'd ever told him in those words. Piecing together their conversations, the information she'd given him about Bagumi and the timing of each revelation, he'd become sure of one thing.

Everything his mother had ever done, the skills she'd encouraged him to acquire, each test and punishment she'd put him through, had all been preparing him for his return to Bagumi, to take his rightful place. Even her death had advanced this cause.

Guilt, a familiar accompaniment to the last thought, slammed into him, indicting him. Surely, he was wrong about that. Mamaa wouldn't rip his heart out in a misguided desire to give him the dream she'd always wanted for him, the connection he no longer sought.

He remembered the letter—his mother's final words to him—which all but confirmed his suspicion.

"Let's have it, then. Your brilliant plan." Shaka's voice reeled him back to the present.

"Which is why it's time for me to visit Bagumi now that they've lifted the travel ban. I need to get closer to him to gather information."

"Going to Bagumi is a dangerous move. Let me do it."

Kal shook his head. His brother might be better skilled at infiltration and surveillance, but he had something Shaka didn't. King Ibrahim Saene's blood.

"If we're to gain access to the palace itself, then it has to be me."

The other man stared at him for a long moment. "Are you sure you want to do this?"

"Mamaa's blood is on King Ibrahim's hands. I can't not do it."

He'd been planning this for nearly a year now, going as far as cultivating the very nations Bagumi had recently fallen out of favour with. Too late to back out.

Standing, he crossed the room to the window and gazed down twelve floors at the hustle and bustle around the Opeibea traffic lights. Rush hour congestion wouldn't thin down for another couple of hours. This was prime time for street hawkers and beggars.

His mind drifted to decades ago when he'd been one of those people. For a moment, the memories poured in unchecked—unending hours under the arduous sun selling chocolate, verbal abuse and inconsideration from motorists while he offered to clean their windscreens in the evenings just for a few coins, fighting off street bullies who tried to steal his money …

Those had been dark times for him and Mamaa. All because her lover had exiled her for the crime of carrying his child.

A sharp pain in his jaw made him realise he was gritting his teeth. He consciously forced himself to relax.

"I need to look the man in the eye when I tell him who I am and how I'm going to make him pay." He returned his gaze to his brother. "I won't be talked out of it."

"After months of trying, I know better." Shaka released a sigh. "I just hope you find what you're really looking for."

He frowned. "What's that supposed to mean?"

"It means don't get yourself killed. There's been enough loss."

The other man's face had taken on a cloak of gravity. The slight cracking of his voice conveyed a message he didn't have to utter.

"I'll be careful," Kal promised.

After several seconds of holding his brother's gaze, he backed down from what might have turned into a staring contest. As he'd hoped, this earned him an acquiescent nod. He released his relief in a breath, his optimism edging up. He'd do this with or without Shaka, but his chances of success would increase exponentially with his brother's expertise.

"Are you sleeping okay?" Shaka asked.

He released an internal groan. "Sleep is overrated."

"You need to see someone about it."

He grimaced. Sometimes, his brother gave mother hens a run for their money. It had gotten worse since Mamaa's passing. Something about a promise she'd extracted from him.

"My mum died. I'm allowed a few sleepless nights."

"For how long?"

"Don't start."

"You need to get laid again. You're overstressed and undersexed."

He shot a warning glare. "Do *not* go there."

He knew Shaka's heart was in the right place. Though they didn't have the same blood running through their veins, Mamaa had dated Shaka's father until the man had perished in a road accident five years later. They'd taken Shaka in, and the two had grown up as brothers.

Hands raised in a conciliatory gesture, Shaka let out an exasperated breath. Thankfully, he knew when to let go.

His own mind, on the other hand, didn't seem to know when to quit. Every sleepless night brought on memories of the brief time since losing Mamaa when he'd slept through several nights. How could he make Shaka understand it hadn't been a result of the physical release? The difference had been *her*. His goddess.

For one glorious week, her calming effect had lingered, bestowing him with the gift of restful slumber and a clear head. That was over now. He didn't appreciate his mind's insistence on replaying their time together in a futile attempt to recapture the elusive sense of peace and belonging.

He shoved the thoughts out of his head. He didn't need the memory of honey eyes messing with his concentration now of all times.

"Once I'm done with King Ibrahim, I'm sure I'll sleep like a baby."

CHAPTER FIVE

The Royal Palace, Kingdom of Umaasie

"Has my fate been decided yet?" Edina asked, her gaze moving from her mother at one end of the large dining table to her brother, the king of Umaasie, at the other end.

Although the table easily sat twelve, they were the only people at dinner. Her mother had requested a private meal with her children tonight.

Requested? Laughable. Her mother summoned, and no one said no to Queen Nataizia.

"Don't be so melodramatic, *Owoahene*," her mum said.

Edina's heart thudded. Some people had started referring to her as *Owoahene*—bearer of kings—soon after her eighteenth birthday when she'd been officially bestowed the honorific title of Princess of the Crown.

Besides the formal ceremony, however, her mother had never referred to her as such before tonight. She also noted how once the food had been served, the staff had exited the room. Normally, they'd stay to serve. Their absence could only mean one thing. The day she dreaded had finally arrived.

Over the past eight months, she'd immersed herself in work, taking on projects that kept her on a busy schedule, leaving little room for socialising. She'd methodically found reasons to disqualify all the suitors paraded before her.

She couldn't blame her lack of an active social life solely on her personal efforts, though. She ascribed equal credit to the coronavirus pandemic, which had swept through the world and changed everything.

Well … not *every*thing, apparently.

She should've known her marriage would return to the fore once the lockdown had been lifted for the sake of those who earned their keep by day. With her thirtieth birthday coming up in less than a year, her leeway would expire soon. If she didn't marry by then, she'd have to share her position as Princess of the Crown with her cousin, Zoraya, since she had no sisters.

Whoever produced an heir first would maintain the title and go on to become queen. As a diarchy, Umaasie was ruled by a king co-reigning with a female member of his lineage. Added to their matrilineal heritage system, the queen also had the responsibility to produce the next heirs to the throne.

She and Zoraya were the oldest of the next generation of future monarchs and queen mothers. Being just a year apart, they'd been playmates growing up. She knew better than most the wickedness that lurked underneath her cousin's beautiful exterior.

Guilt gnawed at her insides. She should never have resisted this long.

She'd based her hopes on an irrational dream—a fantasy that destiny would cross her path with *his* again. Her warrior. She should've known better than to pray for a miracle.

She *did* know better. Sucking in a fortifying breath, she made a pact with herself. She'd accept whoever they proposed, as long as he didn't have any genuinely irredeemable qualities.

Her brother set down his cutlery, the sound interrupting her thoughts. "We're in talks with King Ibrahim Saene of Bagumi."

She released a breath she'd inadvertently been holding. This couldn't be about her marriage since King Ibrahim's sons were all spoken for.

"You must be aware of the discovery of some ancient Bagumian artifacts."

"I am."

Flakes of excitement materialised out of the muddle of worry over the impending marriage alliance, evoking her first real smile of the evening. Discovery of antiquities always thrilled her. There was often something new to learn from history, things which brought a fresh perspective about people who'd existed centuries ago. Somehow, it made her feel connected to something bigger.

"King Ibrahim would like you to be part of a small authentication committee conducting an independent assessment to vouch for their authenticity. He'd also like you to design an exhibition to be held next year for the collection. I trust this is agreeable to you?"

"It is, Brother."

The biennial exhibitions she'd started a few years ago to promote interest in history and disciplines like archaeology and anthropology had been widely successful, garnering international media attention and requests for collaborations from some of the most renowned museums in the world. King Ibrahim's request would be a coup. Her enthusiasm multiplied.

Of course, Bagumi didn't care about her elation. A successful exhibition would boost tourism while changing the narrative of news about the kingdom in international media. After four of King Ibrahim's children had rejected marriage alliances brokered for them, the kingdom had made enemies of several influential nations. Their interest had to be PR-based on some level.

"If I can play a role in preserving peace, then of course, I'm in. In fact, I can't wait to get started."

"Excellent!" Queen Nataizia said. "While you're in Bagumi, you'll use the opportunity to seek the favour of King Ibrahim's son, Azikiwe. He'll officially be named Crown Prince by the end of this month, and we need to know his intentions towards Umaasie. Partnering with Bagumi to develop our mining sector will be better than seeking assistance from the West."

"Not to mention the access to markets we cannot negotiate with on an equal standing," her brother added. "Normally, Mum or I would have done this, but it's not yet safe for us to travel."

She nodded. Her sexagenarian mother and diabetic brother qualified as high-risk. Despite all the safety precautions they'd instituted to keep themselves and citizens safe, without a cure or vaccine, it was best to stay safe.

"It's time I took on a more active public role as a senior royal of Umaasie, anyway," she said. "Isn't that what you're always saying?"

She instantly regretted her words when her mother beamed. Had she walked straight into a trap?

"I'm so happy to hear that. Your father would have been so proud of the woman you've become."

Grief washed over her as it did every time she thought about the man who'd been taken from them much too soon. Echoes of sorrow in her mother's eyes told her the woman still missed him. In those few seconds when their gazes met in acknowledgment of their loss, she felt a connection to her mother she hadn't experienced in years.

The meal continued with general conversation, and for several moments, they were like any ordinary family around a dinner table. It had been so long since she'd spent this much time with her mother and brother without royal matters overtaking the discussion. Her father had been the one who kept them focused, reminded his son and wife there was more to life than the throne.

When the main course ended, she declined dessert. Dinner had been wonderful, but she'd spent most of her day in virtual meetings, including some with students of a class she taught at the University of Umaasie. Who knew sitting all day could be exhausting?

"May I be excused?" she said.

"Are you sure you don't want to try this gari cake? Cook has outdone herself today," her mother said.

"I'm sure." She'd never had a sweet tooth, and normally ate her fruits at the beginning of her meals whenever possible as she'd done today. "I've had a long day, and I'd like to turn in early. Besides, if I'm to travel to Bagumi, I need to start preparing."

She began to stand.

"Before you go," her brother started.

A sinking feeling registered in her gut.

He pinned her with a look, not speaking until she'd lowered herself back on the chair.

"Have you chosen a suitor yet?"

She stifled a groan. *So close.*

"I thought I had until the end of the week."

Her mother cleared her throat, pulling on her impenetrable cloak of stoicism. Whatever she said next would be as queen rather than mother.

"Not anymore. If you haven't selected among the list of perfectly good candidates by now, what's another couple of days going to do? I'm going to make things simple for you."

Her heart clenched. She didn't like the sound of it. "What do you mean?"

"I'm taking the decision from you," her mother replied. "We'll choose, and you must accept."

"Mum!"

Her mother raised a hand to silence her. "I've tried to be patient with you, Edina. I gave you something neither I nor your brother had. Time and options. Clearly, I made a mistake, because it seems you think I'll sit quietly by and watch you deprive my descendants of the throne."

Amazing how her mother could sound composed while delivering a threat. She didn't respond, hoping her silence would earn her some consideration, because her mother didn't issue idle threats.

"Luckily," the older woman continued. "I have the perfect candidate. He's an Ashanti sub-chief, a member of parliament in Ghana, and doing great things for his country. You've actually met him before. Nana Kwame Siriboe II."

She frowned. "Who?"

"That's his throne name," her brother responded. "He's known in private life as Mathew Osei Wusu."

The name did sound vaguely familiar, but for the life of her, she couldn't place him.

"His father and I are old friends, and he has my permission to woo you." The queen's tone brooked no argument.

It hit her then. This 'quiet' dinner had been orchestrated to steamroll her with this news. She turned to her brother, hoping for ... what? Sympathy? She got a look that said fighting would be a futile venture. Instead, he delivered the deathblow.

"As soon as you return from Bagumi, you'll satisfy the three-month courtship and marry."

If she wasn't schooled in diplomacy, she'd have been picking her jaw from the polished marble floor. Instead, she clenched her teeth. Her body went rigid, and her heart pounded. It took all her willpower to prevent her lips from quivering and tears from forming. Still unable to believe he'd delivered his little speech with a straight face and an unwavering voice, she stared at her brother—her *king*.

She didn't know what hurt more: how he'd always seemed to be on her side from the start, or that she'd allowed herself to believe she might have some wiggle room in this whole situation. Worse, he'd buttered her up by dangling the bit about the antiquities before her. Like a naïve little fish, she'd swallowed it hook, line, and sinker.

At the end of the day, Barimah had proven to be first and foremost a king. Shame on her for not realising this before.

Her head and heart warred, one pulling her towards submission, the other in the direction of defiance. Given the epic failure of her last attempt at rebellion, obedience seemed to be the appropriate option. This was, after all, what it meant to put country before self.

"As you wish, Your Majesty." Her voice came out flat, unfeeling.

To her surprise, her mother's expression softened. "He'd make a fine match, *Owoahene*. He's of noble birth, an esteemed politician, and a successful entrepreneur. He says you met at a charity event in Abidjan a couple of years ago and you two hit it off. He speaks highly of you."

She grimaced, now remembering the man. He was indeed accomplished, respected from the little she knew of him in the news. She had to admit, she'd found him good-looking, until ten minutes into their conversation, he'd declared, "Now that you're in my heart, you should stay there." His cheesy line and subsequent show of arrogance had been a major turn-off. When he'd asked her out on a date, she'd declined.

"No man is perfect, my daughter," her mother said. "With a good man, love will grow in time."

She opened her mouth to protest when she remembered her silent promise to accept whoever they proposed, if he didn't have any genuinely irredeemable qualities. Somehow, she didn't think she could disqualify him based on his pomposity and lack of game.

She swallowed past the sudden lump in her throat. "If your due diligence hasn't unearthed any skeletons in his closet, then I'll accept his suit."

What was there to lose? No man would ever hold a candle to her warrior.

"It hurts me when you get that look in your eyes," Barimah said.

"What look?"

"The one which says you think you'll never be happy again."

Well, that summed up her feelings succinctly. The reality of it stung, but choice—love—and, therefore happiness, wasn't an option available to her.

"Have Mahalia and I set such a bad example?"

She had to smile. Anyone who saw the way Barimah doted on his wife would never suspect they hadn't met in person until a few weeks to their wedding.

"Mahalia was pledged to you from a young age. She had time to be groomed into the woman of your dreams."

Even to her ears, it sounded ridiculous. Her brother and his wife were so well-matched and completely in love, she had no doubt they'd somehow have gravitated towards each other even without the betrothal. They had the real thing. Something she could forget about for herself.

"It's not as bad as you seem to imagine," her mother said, concern briefly knotting between her brows.

Except that it was. She'd never experience being loved and loving back. Prior to eight months ago, she'd imagined the sex at least would be good, when she'd had nothing to compare it with. The warrior had changed that. With one look, one touch, one whisper … one night, he'd marked her as his. Yet, she had no idea about his identity. She'd been the one to insist on anonymity, but how much of a risk would it have been to simply know his name?

She'd tried to move on. It had been the plan all along. She'd even been amenable to the interest of her suitors, going out with several. However, every date—every kiss—had just confirmed what she'd suspected. No other man's touch would make her feel so thoroughly complete. For once, the woman in her had taken precedence over the princess.

It had been a monumental mistake. Whatever chances she'd had of a marginally happy marriage, owing to blissful ignorance of the ways of a man with a woman, had been dashed by the acts of a few hours.

As the memories flooded her mind, her tummy flipped, and desire detonated in her core. The sudden, intense sensation nearly made her moan.

"Are you all right?" her brother asked.

One would think after all these months, she'd be used to it. Thoughts of him, no matter how brief, sent her in a whorl of need that took her by surprise. Every time.

"I'm fine," she lied, reaching for her half-full water goblet and taking a long sip.

Heat of embarrassment layered over that from passion, and suddenly, all she wanted was to get to her chambers and take off every single item of clothing weighing down on her. She wanted to be as naked as she'd been when he'd touched her and made her body bloom into womanhood.

And also psych herself for her imminent engagement. She didn't voice that thought.

"May I be excused now?" She stood, making it clear she didn't intend to be talked out of leaving.

Barimah nodded. Without another word, she started walking, praying her legs weren't too wobbly to carry her to her chambers where she could capitulate to her emotions.

CHAPTER SIX

Darusa, Capital city of Bagumi

Kalahari fiddled with the ring his mother had given him on his eighteenth birthday. It bore the royal seal of the House of Saene, but he hadn't known its significance until recently.

"Guard it with jealousy, Rahim. You'll need it someday," she'd told him while pressing it into his palm.

She'd used that moniker whenever they'd had a serious conversation. Though Rahim wasn't a diminutive of his middle name—Ibrahim—it served the purpose between them.

He'd kept it in a wooden box where he hid his most prized possessions, things whose value couldn't be counted in monetary terms but meant the world to him. She hadn't mentioned the ring again until a couple of days before she'd died. It had been after their usual weekly dinner.

She'd talked about her days as a palace staff in Bagumi, about being elevated from Ladies' Maid to Governess following the birth of Prince Zawadi. She'd told him about a grotto where she and his father used to spend time.

"Swear to me you'll spread my ashes there when I die," she'd said.

He hadn't wanted to think about her and death in the same sentence. She'd persisted despite his refusals and eventually secured a promise from him.

"Do you still have the ring, Rahim?" she'd asked. "Take it with you. The king shall fulfil his word if you show him the ring."

Forty-eight hours later, his world had changed.

She still hadn't told him the king and his father were the same person. No. She'd let him discover that in the letter.

Letters, he corrected. One to him and a dozen to the man she'd loved. He'd discovered those in her bedroom safe, letters that sought to update his father about their lives, reminders of promises unfulfilled, declaration of her love. Each one ended the same. *'I miss you every day.'* The last, dated just six months earlier, had been different, the tone accusatory, signed *'Til we meet again.'*

He jerked out of the memories which would surely haunt him for the rest of his life. Better to focus on the next couple of weeks. Mentally, he went over his programme. While researching Bagumi and its ruler, he'd come across news about the discovery of a substantial deposit of ancient Bagumian artifacts of significance to the royal family.

He'd immediately seen the opportunity it presented. Given how old some of the items were reported to be, most would need some amount of refurbishment. Such restoration didn't come cheap. Granted, King Ibrahim had more than enough money to spare, but the ability to attract independent funding lent a measure of authenticity in the eyes of other donors and societies.

He'd wasted no time in submitting an expression of interest in the name of the Asanti Foundation, the charitable wing of his organisation, to fund the exercise. He'd even thrown in a section on sustainability, outlining a plan to ensure continued funding over the long-term. His Bagumian roots had come in handy in explaining his motivation.

To make it an offer King Ibrahim couldn't refuse, he'd ensured his proposal outshone any other offers.

Over the years, he'd perfected information trading to an art. Some called it blackmail. He found the term distasteful and too simplistic to cover what he did. He wasn't above employing dirty tricks to achieve his ends, but even when he derived personal gain from his actions, his motivation was never about himself. He fought for the little guy, which he'd once been. This situation was no different.

As the undertaking seemed to be important to the king, Kal had hoped to be granted an audience with him. His plan had worked even better than expected. The invitation had arrived a week ago. It bore the king's seal and an invitation for Kal to stay at the palace as a guest.

Not bad for the son of a palace maid.

He couldn't have hoped for a better turn of events. Whatever consequences Ibrahim had feared so much that he'd preferred to exile a pregnant woman, Kal would bring upon his unworthy royal head. The man should count himself lucky this was all he had in store for him, because what Ibrahim deserved would be to have his heart ripped out and witness it being crushed.

Blood for blood. It was the only thing capable of attempting to blot out the image of Mamaa when he'd found her on the bathroom floor clutching to life by a thread—a life she'd decided was no longer worth living.

She'd had her moments, days where her mood fluctuated from high to low in seconds. But she'd always had ways of dealing with it, most of the time channelling her lows into her fashion designing. Whenever he'd urged her to take things slow, she'd wave him off with her standard reply.

"Creative people are highly in touch with their emotions. It's when we do our best work."

He should never have taken her word for it. He'd seen her for dinner once every week for years. He should have known she'd been suffering in silence. How could he not have seen it?

He slammed the shutters down on the thoughts, diverting his attention to the panorama below as the chartered plane approached the Darusa International Airport. Staring at the undulating hills, he couldn't help admiring the lush greenery punctuated by industrial buildings. They soon transitioned into estate-type residential and commercial properties. The runway came into view as the pilot announced touchdown in five minutes. Taxiing didn't take long as the flight had been cleared to land in a private section of the airport.

Upon disembarkation, a uniformed chauffeur met him on the tarmac with a limited-edition Mercedes S-class bearing the royal crest. The emblem was also emblazoned on his breast pocket and the black nose mask.

"I am under instruction to convey you to the palace, Mr Asanti," the driver said after introducing himself as Hakeem. "I'll be your driver for the duration of your stay."

He'd taken the obligatory PCR test before gaining permission to travel to Bagumi, but he was still required to take an Antigen Qualitative Test to confirm he didn't have an active coronavirus infection—a necessary precaution for any visitors, but especially for people seeking audience with the king.

They were on their way in less than forty minutes, the least time Kal had ever spent at an airport where he wasn't a returning resident. The many perks of being a royal guest, he supposed.

As they drove, he couldn't help feeling a sense of familiarity. Must have been all that time he'd spent studying Bagumi in preparation for this trip. As far as he knew, his mother had never brought him here.

He suspected Hakeem had used the scenic route, taking it upon himself to point out a few landmarks on the way.

"You sound proud of Bagumi," Kal noted.

"Yes, sir," the driver said. "It's a beautiful and peaceful place. A land of opportunity."

For several minutes, he listened to the man talk about moving his family here from Nigeria twenty years ago. With a Cameroonian wife and families on both sides against the marriage, Bagumi had seemed like a good middle ground.

He frowned as something caught his interest. The streets were pristine. They'd been driving for nearly an hour and hadn't encountered one street hawker or beggar. The lack of visible poverty might impress some, but to him, it raised a red flag. The statistics might not be as dire as in Lagos, Accra, or Johannesburg, but as an upper middle-income country, Bagumi wasn't immune to the scourge of homelessness.

"What happened to the street vendors?"

In the rear-view mirror, he saw Hakeem's eyes crinkle at the corners, suggesting a smile concealed by the nose mask. A guilty smile, no doubt, given his entire speech so far had reeked of tourist spiel.

"They've been moved."

He frowned. "By whom?"

"The palace started an exercise last year to clear the streets of vendors and homeless people."

"Really?"

"Yes, sir. An ambitious project, too. They're giving affordable or free housing, employment or training in a vocation."

On the surface, low-cost housing and employment appeared to be steps in the right direction. From his own experience, he knew most general efforts to remove people from the streets tended to be for PR mileage. They never had a long-term view nor did they truly address the real reasons putting people on the streets to begin with.

He'd witnessed many such campaigns victimising the very people they were meant to help.

He made a mental note to investigate the project. If it turned out to be a genuine campaign, it might present an opportunity for another Asanti Foundation's project, Kalahari's Kids, which aimed at sustainable rehabilitation of street children and their families in the cities where he did business. With the country still under partial lockdown, travel between city lines was restricted. He'd have to do what he could remotely and hope life returned to a semblance of normalcy soon.

"Do you like working for the royal family?" he asked at the first opportunity to interject.

"Oh, yes," came the response. "King Ibrahim is a good leader and a good boss. Without him, we wouldn't be where we are today."

He supposed the man had to have some redeeming qualities for Mamaa to fall for him and continue to love him despite his repudiation. As a child, he'd yearned for the hero his mother had made him out to be. As he'd grown older, however, her devotion to the man who'd never graced their lives with an appearance had made less and less sense. It didn't fit with the woman he'd known as his mother, the woman who'd risen from improbable beginnings as palace staff in a tiny African kingdom to become a gem in the fashion world. Her label catered exclusively to the wealthy, making a name and fortune for herself while remaining out of the public eye.

Unwilling to descend down the rabbit hole of memories, he shifted his thoughts back to the scenery outside. Darusa was undeniably beautiful. As in many African capital cities, its architecture juxtaposed old and ultra-modern, with influences from various cultures and historical eras. Unlike some, though, the city was very green; not in the manicured way common in the developed world, but in a manner suggesting some effort had been put into preserving the natural environment. It enhanced the beauty of the landscape.

His mind drifted to another occasion when a mix of cultures had been intricately woven together to create a masterpiece. The face of a goddess veiled by tribal tattoos, vivid African gemstones sewn onto the softest imported silk and a sprinkle of crystals. His fingers tingled with the memory of touching her, holding her ...

He shut his eyes, briefly indulging in the recollection of a woman who'd branded him without revealing as much as her name.

He tore his eyes open. What was wrong with him? He'd arrived in Bagumi, closer than he'd ever been to King Ibrahim, closer than he'd ever come to avenging his mother. Instead of strategizing, he was thinking about a woman. By God. Her magic must be more potent than he'd imagined. Perhaps knowing nothing about her had been fortunate.

Time to banish thoughts of his night with a goddess once and for all.

The palace was a fair drive from the airport. If he didn't occupy his mind, he might find himself drifting back into the goddess' trap. To ensure he didn't, he continued to engage Hakeem in conversation, which seemed to please the friendly chauffeur.

"The palace is up ahead."

The driver's announcement drew Kal's gaze up to the palatial structure emerging behind a fortress of vegetation. Like many castles built in the eras of war, the edifice sat on a hill where the palace guards would spot invaders ahead of time.

They drove up a stone-paved driveway framed by large tropical trees that had to be centuries old judging by their size. They reached an unmanned gate, which slid open to allow them entry. Then, they encountered a second gate a couple of minutes later, this one with two security men at post to perform standard checks.

Past the gate, the driveway opened out into the palace square. The building stood a few yards ahead, vast and imposing. He'd seen photos, but it appeared even more impressive. Somehow, the pictures had failed to capture the majesty of its design—another mixture of cultures depicted in the architecture.

It reminded him of his mother's clothing line, Yadira Designs, which always paid tribute to her Bagumian roots.

He brought his mind back to the present. The last thing he needed was to be raw with emotion when he met King Ibrahim. The man couldn't know of the animosity Kal harboured against him. He had to maintain the element of surprise in order to execute his mission to the fullest extent.

As the vehicle came to a stop, the driver turned. "I am taking your luggage to your suite, but I'll be back to pick you after your meeting with His Majesty."

"Very well," Kal said, exiting the car.

Any compromising document he had was in his cloud, so he didn't worry about the safety of his belongings.

A palace official met him at the entrance and ushered him into a waiting area where another staff member briefed him on protocols for meeting the king. Fifteen minutes later, he was led out of the room and through a corridor. CCTV cameras and guards at vantage points confirmed the heightened security at the palace since an assassination attempt made on Prince Zawadi several months ago.

They entered a room which turned out to be a front office for the king's secretary. The door to the king's office was unmanned from this end, but when they entered, two guards stood at each side of the double door. They looked meaner than any of the ones he'd encountered.

He'd met a few heads of state, and as presidential offices went, this was pretty standard. It was a large space, opulent in its décor. He'd never be comfortable working daily from this room. The fixtures in his offices across the globe may be expensive by regular standards, but the emphasis had always been on quality and comfort. He'd seen enough of the other side of the coin to rub his wealth in anyone's face.

His gaze moved from the House of Saene coat of arms in the centre of the carpet to the king seated at a massive desk at the far end. The sight of the other man stopped him for several seconds as he stared into eyes so similar to his. A chill rushed up his spine, leaving him in no doubt the same blood ran through their veins. He waited for the hate to surface, the foremost emotion he'd nursed in relation to the man seated before him. All he could muster was a raging curiosity.

"Mr Asanti," the king said, standing. "Good afternoon, and welcome to Bagumi."

The king wore an elaborate robe, which Kal immediately identified as a traditional Bagumian outfit. Even if he hadn't seen less stylish versions earlier on the drive from the airport, the Bagumian identity in his mother's designer clothing would have clued him in.

There he went again, thinking about Mamaa. Was that her way of showing disapproval for his plans?

He stopped in the middle of the room, just off the crest as protocol demanded. Normally, the monarch would have had to meet the guest as a sign of welcome. In less civil times, a person could lose their heads for getting too close to the seat of power without permission. He had no doubt the two guards wouldn't hesitate to put a bullet through his head if he so much as breathed the wrong way.

Observing the mandatory social distancing protocol, the king didn't approach.

"Your Majesty," he said, bowing low while invoking a blessing on the older man in impeccable Bagumese.

"You are Bagumian," he remarked as Kal straightened to his full height.

"By blood."

He considered himself a citizen of Africa. His maternal grandmother had been Bagumian, but his mother's father had been from Ghana, while Shaka's father had been Zambian. Growing up, they'd lived in several countries across the continent. Now, he understood Mamaa must have been on the move so often because she'd been running.

"Blood is one of the strongest bonds there is," the king said. "It's what has brought you here, is it not? After all, there are many support-worthy causes in every country in the world."

"But no other country has you for a king."

Ibrahim let out a hearty laugh, clearly taking the remark as a compliment.

"My mother always told me stories about Bagumi and its royal family."

"Your parents never brought you?"

"She had no family left in the country, and while she loved Bagumi a lot, she also had sad memories from her life here."

Why the hell had he said that? He'd promised himself not to reveal anything personal, but here he was already breaking that rule.

"I hope you'll have a better experience."

"I intend to, Your Majesty."

Their gazes held briefly, and the king paused as if studying him. He did the same. The monarch then sat, thus giving him permission to follow suit. Once seated, King Ibrahim launched into the discussion with a little background.

"Bagumi has a rich cultural heritage. Our arts and crafts were sought after long before modern civilisation," he began. "Although we were never colonised, we're a small nation with a lot of natural resources. These two facts alone made us attractive to invaders. Consequently, the crown lost a significant amount of its riches through wars. Part of our strength has historically been in the support of bigger, more powerful nations."

Kal nodded, although most of this wasn't news to him.

"During my grandfather's reign, the crown sought to reclaim some of the kingdom's lost treasures, including legally obtaining them from collectors. As you can imagine, this didn't come cheap. The discovery of these new artifacts on Bagumian soil is most significant. The timing couldn't be better as Bagumi is at a place where the crown needs to regain the people's trust."

"You're talking about Prince Zawadi's abdication?"

The monarch paused as if he hadn't expected the interruption. However, if he felt slighted, he didn't show it.

"He was our beloved Crown Prince. To some, he still is."

A beat passed as the king backtracked to his introduction. Once that ended, he opened the floor for Kal to speak.

Kal then went over the proposal he'd drafted a small team from the company to develop. For Asanti Foundation, this would be a genuine project, but for him personally, it was a means to an end. As he went through his spiel, the king asked a lot of questions, and gave input intermittently. The meeting lasted a little over an hour, ending with a mutually agreeable plan.

The king stood, and Kal followed.

"Since you're staying at the palace, I insist you have breakfast with me."

He readily accepted the invitation. The meeting couldn't have gone better. He'd jumped the first hurdle. He had a foot in the door.

CHAPTER SEVEN

Kal touched base with Shaka before getting ready for the first item on his agenda for the day— breakfast with the king at seven. As he'd told him, things couldn't have gotten off to a better start. He still needed to keep his instincts on high alert, though. He couldn't afford any missteps while in Bagumi.

At six-forty, Hakeem picked him up and dropped him off at the appropriate entrance. It appeared to be a different wing from where he'd had the meeting yesterday.

A man who looked to be in his mid-forties met them at the door. "Thank you, Hakeem. I'll lead Mr Asanti to the breakfast room."

Hakeem tipped his hat, and Kal acknowledged it with a nod before following the butler through a corridor exhibiting portraits of past Bagumian rulers. Given his mother's relationship with the king, he guessed she'd once walked through here. A sense of closeness with her enveloped him. He revelled in the emotion for a moment before putting a clamp on it. He didn't want Mamaa in his head appealing to his good sense when he needed to feed his rage.

They arrived at a door, which the butler opened while announcing him.

Kal entered. The morning sun poured in through windows overlooking a large flower garden. His gaze swept over the nook on his right with a buffet layout that rivalled any he'd seen at the five-star hotels he'd stayed at.

Seated at the sixteen-seater breakfast table, the king looked up from a newspaper. "Mr Asanti, please come in. The others should arrive shortly."

Others?

As though he'd read Kal's mind, he explained, "I have breakfast with my children each day. As many of them as are available. With their busy schedules, if I don't insist on this, I might not see some of them for weeks. The pandemic has changed things, though, so today it's going to be just Azikiwe with a guest."

He gestured to a seat. "Please. Sit."

Kal sat down.

"You're welcome to have a cup of tea or coffee while we wait," the king offered, taking a sip from a teacup in front of him.

"Just water. Thank you."

The king motioned to one of two house staff in the room who immediately came to serve Kal. He waited until the server had stepped away before taking off his nose mask and folding it into his pocket.

"I hope you're hungry, Mr Asanti."

"Kal, please."

"Why do you cut your name short? Kalahari suits you much better," the king said, studying him the way he had yesterday. "Your tough exterior masks a kaleidoscope of raw emotions. Reminds me of a young me."

Funny, his mother had said the same, which had fanned his anger. He hadn't been sure who he was angry with. Mamaa for trying to reverse his disillusionment about his father, or said father for never showing up. There were many aspects of his character he definitely didn't get from his mother. Intellectually, he knew they had to be from his father—from Ibrahim—which pissed him off even more.

"If you don't mind, I'll call you Kalahari." Not a request, Kal noted. "I trust you had a good first day."

"I did, and I look forward to the museum visit this morning."

"As you should. We have a good collection there. As an investor, you'll get to see where your money's going. Reassuring stakeholders is imperative to building trust." The king waved a hand. "No more business talk. I want to know more about you. Do you have a family?"

He had no interest in being friendly with the king. As much as perceived friendship would make retribution cut deeper, he couldn't stomach the idea of even pretending to like Ibrahim no matter how convincing the man's act of friendliness—a salesman's tactics as far as he was concerned. No, he was here on a mission. Undercover, even.

"I have a foster brother, but no family of my own at the moment."

"Family is important," Ibrahim said.

"Is that why you tried to arrange marriages for your children, if I may be bold enough to ask?"

"Ah, so the news is out there."

"I did my homework."

"Besides blood, marriage is the next indestructible bond that has stood the test of time."

"I would think in the twenty-first century that countries might have found ways of creating alliances without making it a burden on people of royal birth."

The older man sighed. "Alas, royal intermarriages aren't going away anytime soon. Once in a while, the union is catastrophic, but if you choose well, the chances of love blooming increases exponentially."

He quirked his brows. Several of Ibrahim's children had already chosen different paths. He'd expected the king to hold a modified opinion.

"Despite the partial lockdown, I hope you'll take advantage of the good weather we're having and explore more of Bagumi's sights and culinary offerings," the king said, changing the subject. "If there's anything I can do to make your stay more pleasant, don't hesitate to ask."

"There is one thing." He'd wondered the best time to make this request, but since Ibrahim had asked. "I'd like permission to bury my mother."

"Oh, I didn't realise ..." The man's smile dimmed. "I'm sorry for your loss."

He accepted the compliment with reverence to his mother.

"Bagumi may be a monarchy, but you don't need the king's permission to bury your mother here, even if she weren't a citizen."

"I do need to ask because of where she wants to be buried."

"Oh?"

"A grotto on the palace grounds," he said. "Named after the queen of the king's heart."

At his words, the king stilled, his demeanour becoming solemn. Kal's pulse surged. Perhaps he should have been more tactful. But he didn't have the luxury of time. He'd just have to weather whatever storm he may have set off.

"Who's your mother?"

"From the look on your face, Your Majesty, I think you know exactly who she was. However, if you must hear it, she was called Yara Asanti, and she used to work for you."

King Ibrahim let out a heavy breath, nodding.

"You're Yara's son," he stated in a low voice, which seemed to have struggled to find its way out. "And your father?"

Don't you recognise your own son?

"I never knew him," he answered, keeping his voice unemotional, his gaze unwavering.

A lesser man would have flinched, but Ibrahim didn't back down for several seconds.

"You've turned out a fine young man regardless."

Before he had a chance to respond, the doors opened, drawing their attention.

"Azikiwe, come on in. I'd like you to meet Mr Kalahari Asanti, the man interested in sponsoring our newly discovered artifacts. I think you two will get along quite well."

Kal stood to acknowledge the prince.

"Pleasure to meet you, Mr Asanti," Prince Azikiwe said. "And it's Zik. Only Father calls me by my full name."

Smiling, he said, "Kal."

Next to Azikiwe stood—

He blinked.

Her?

By God! Was he seeing things?

His gaze met honey eyes, and a shudder slammed into him, birthing a tingling in his spine. Within an instant, his entire back began to prickle. The world started spinning dangerously out of control, and he found himself needing an anchor. Luckily, his hand rested on the back of the chair. He firmed his grip.

Only one person had ever had that kind of effect on him. She had her nose mask on, but he didn't need to see her entire face to identify her.

She froze as recognition poured into her eyes, causing them to widen with her surprise. His mind called back the memory of staring into them while making love with her, of the way they'd flared with passion and wonder as her body had tightened around him …

This could be an ambush. The stark reality of the moment occurred, but it didn't douse the inferno the sight of her had ignited. It took sheer force of self-preservation to bring his mind under enough control to achieve a semblance of thought. He'd suspected her of being a spy, and then dismissed it by checking off a list of possibilities. He'd believed in his instincts, which had never steered him wrong. A testament to her skills as a master of deception.

The truth could be far worse. He remembered the king's words. *Azikiwe and a guest.* Were they in a relationship? Had she cheated on her boyfriend with him? Revulsion filled him. He'd never have touched her if he'd known she was taken.

Zik placed what he could only interpret as a possessive hand on her back. No mistaking the intent. He hadn't reined in his desires quickly enough, and he'd given the man reason to get territorial.

Merde.

"I'd like to present Her Royal Highness Princess Edina Masira Dampare."

Princess?

It took him a couple more seconds to recover his wits.

He dipped his head and murmured, "*Enchanté.*"

***

Edina stared into eyes she'd dreamed about every night for eight months. In the daylight, his dark-grey irises had a silvery gleam in them. They were even more arresting than she recalled, more intense. Yet, they held none of the warmth or humour.

He couldn't be here, couldn't be real. Not when she'd agreed to a courtship upon her return to Umaasie.

Could she go through with the engagement? It had been easy to accept her fate when she hadn't known the warrior's identity, when the possibility of seeing him again had been nil. She'd convinced herself everything she'd felt that night had been due to it being her first time. Her reaction to him now laid bare that lie.

Calling up several of her mother's mantras, she managed to remain steady, forcing her eyes to maintain his gaze without betraying her thoughts.

"*Enchantée*," she finally replied.

His name reverberated in her head.

Kalahari.

It fit him as perfectly as his designer suit. Although, no item of clothing would ever surpass his smooth, dark-chocolate skin. She remembered how she'd feasted her eyes on him when he'd stood naked before her, how bold she'd been to explore the perfection of his body with her hands and lips, how she'd relished her effect on him however temporary.

Oh! Guilt blazed her face. She shouldn't covet him. Her future husband was no longer a nameless, faceless person. Though for the life of her, she couldn't even remember his name right now. *Shameful.*

For all she knew, this man had been sent that night to test her virtue, a test she'd so thoroughly failed. She'd been easy prey, a sheltered princess bent on defying the rules encumbering her. Perhaps it didn't take a stretch of the imagination to figure out she'd be drawn to the tall, dark loner who'd seemed like he didn't want to be there.

If so, then his presence here couldn't be a coincidence. Had he known her identity all along?

Had he come here to discredit her? Forestall the trade alliance? What did he have to gain from either? Did he come on his own behalf or someone else's?

On the heel of that thought, a chilling possibility occurred. Had he recorded their actions? Suddenly, she couldn't breathe. She gasped, reaching for something to hold on to. Her hand raked the air without finding anything solid to grab. The next instant, arms closed around her.

His.

Kalahari's.

Heat from his hands seared her through her blouse. Her head jerked up. Almost immediately, he released her as if the contact with her had burnt him. He'd felt it, too.

"Forgive me," he said. "I wasn't thinking."

"Are you all right?" Zik asked at the same time, concern in his eyes.

She forced a smile. "I must be hungrier than I thought."

Apparently, she was a better liar than she imagined because he seemed satisfied with her response. At any rate, he didn't get the chance to probe.

"Now that we're all here, let's eat," King Ibrahim declared.

She took in several discreet breaths to compose herself. Hopefully, focusing on the meal would defuse the forcefield radiating from Kalahari.

The seating arrangement didn't help. The king and Zik sat at either end of the large dining table with Kalahari opposite her. How was she expected to get through breakfast when she had to meet his eyes every time she looked up?

Forcing her food down with freshly squeezed orange juice provided enough distraction to keep her gaze from wandering across the table to where Kalahari sat, having a conversation with Zik. She interjected every now and then purely on autopilot. Just when her heartbeat seemed to return to normal, the king mentioned Kalahari's name, and every effort she'd made to calm her heart became instantly pointless.

"As I've already mentioned, Kalahari's foundation is interested in sponsoring the restoration work and exhibition of our new artifacts."

Her heart thudded. *He* was her lunch engagement? It kept getting worse! Yet, her plan to excuse herself from lunch began to waver.

"Edina," the king addressed her, forcing her mind back to his words. "Kalahari will be joining you on your trip to the museum after breakfast."

Unavoidably, her gaze shot to the subject of the conversation. Their gazes collided. He smiled despite the calculating look in his eyes. Her heart continued to pump an erratic tempo, though she couldn't tell whether it was due to her increasing apprehension or excitement at seeing him again.

"So I'm not the only one attracted to your new collection?" he said, returning his gaze to King Ibrahim.

"No nothing like that. I invited Princess Edina to be part of an authentication committee and also to design an exhibition for the collection." King

Ibrahim smiled. "She's an anthropologist with a sterling reputation. She'll be able to answer any technical questions you may have during your visit."

Kalahari's gaze returned to her. "I'm sure she will."

"One of our protocol staff has been assigned to you for as long as you need her."

"Very kind of you, Your Majesty."

"I've asked her to show you around the city. You won't mind that small unscheduled activity added to your programme, would you?"

With a brief upturn of his lips, Kalahari answered, "I'd be honoured."

"Perfect."

Was it just her, or had she seen a twinkle in the king's eye? Something twinged in her chest. Who was this protocol staff? Could King Ibrahim be playing cupid? She shook herself mentally. None of her business.

So why did she have half a mind to thwart whatever matchmaking plans the king had?

Like a moth to flame, her gaze drifted over to him. Who was he? What were his real reasons for being in Bagumi? Had he been paid to spy on her? She'd have to find a way of getting him alone at some point during the museum visit in order to query him. Meeting him here couldn't be an act of coincidence. Could it?

CHAPTER EIGHT

Edina sighed relief when breakfast ended. As they dispersed, she made a pointed decision not to look in Kalahari's direction. After one hour's exposure to him, she needed time to regroup before subjecting her senses to another onslaught of his heated gaze, especially given her intention of confronting him at the earliest opportunity.

The thought of lunch with him had her pulse racing. She made a beeline to the ladies' room, needing some alone time to compose herself before facing him again. A cursory inspection of her lavender silk blouse and midi-length batik print skirt brought a measure of calm. Her long braids, swept back in a half up-do to keep them from her face, remained as they should.

Taking off her nose mask, she applied a fresh coat of her plum red matte lipstick and waited half a minute before blotting it. To minimise the risk of staining her mask, she decided to wait until she was in public before putting it on again. Buoyed with the satisfaction of having nailed her chic-but-practical look, she pivoted on her wedge-heeled sandals and headed out.

She found Kalahari already in the waiting room, his back to the door. No sign of anyone else.

Hesitation glued her to the threshold while lust had her taking in his magnificent masculinity as he leaned forward to study a painting of a young African girl who appeared to be commanding a storm. The girl's look of calm confidence in her considerable power gave her goosebumps. If only *she* had the same kind of strength to master the storm brewing around her.

Despite the beauty of the piece, her eyes lingered over the slashes and symmetries of his impossibly fit physique. With both hands pocketed, his trousers moulded scandalously around his firm behind, causing her breath to hitch in her throat. *Good Lord!*

She rushed her attention to a lesser threat to her sanity—the undulation of muscles under his shirt sleeves. Was this how they'd rippled when he'd leaned over her?

Her imaginings screeched to an abrupt end when she remembered their night together—her one moment of folly—may have been immortalised on video by the very man she couldn't stop lusting after. Was he the kind of person who'd sell to the highest bidder? With the right audience, he could destroy the fragile fabric of her country's governance.

Better to handle the situation now before it got to that. The question was how. What would it take to make him go away?

The door hadn't made a sound when she'd opened it, but in shutting, the nose settled in with a soft click. He turned around. A slow smile gained on his lips, his manner a little too casual, and she realised he must have been aware of her entry, fully cognisant of her shameless admiration.

She shuttered down the thoughts and focused on what to say. *Who are you, and what's your business in Bagumi?* Those were the words she wanted to say, but she needed to be tactful. She didn't have the luxury of a second chance.

Her gaze slipped past him to the painting. "It's beautiful."

He quirked his brows as unabashed interest filled his dark grey eyes. "Breathtaking."

With the one word, he increased the surrounding temperature and charged every cell in her body, effectively shifting the dynamics of the room. Her heartbeat surged. Nerves twisted around her insides. And she'd thought she had control, that somehow her suspicions gave her an advantage. Surprise factor? *Ha!* If there were an upper hand in this scenario, it rested firmly in his large hands.

"We meet again." His smile didn't reach his eyes. "So, you and Prince Azikiwe."

Wait. He thought she was dating Zik?

"Congratulations."

Those happy words belied the tempest in his eyes, a look that predicted total destruction to whomever stood in his path. Right now, it was her.

Her first instinct was to correct him, then she realised it didn't matter. In three months, she'd be a married woman. She opted to neither confirm nor deny, but focus on finding out whether he was a threat to her or her country.

Silence hung uncomfortably between them, begging to be filled, and she found herself explaining, "I didn't expect to meet you again."

He approached her with the deliberate, graceful strides of a man who held all the aces. She wanted to shake off his immobilising effect on her, but her attempt proved futile. Like prey caught in the snare of a predator, she took refuge in the distance between them.

"Would it have made a difference?"

A loaded question. She didn't seek clarification, because she knew exactly what he meant. Would she have followed him to the balcony that night? Gone with him to the hotel? Since her choice of a husband wasn't entirely up to her, there could only be one answer. She shook her head.

"Then you were looking for a prince, after all." A beat passed. "Is he aware he wasn't your first? I know how dearly some people hold such trivialities."

Her heart lurched. His words confirmed he had negative intentions. Disappointment descended on her, drenching her in regret—for her actions that night, yes, but more for the consequences bound to befall her people if the truth came out and the alliance fell through as a result. Anger rose.

"You're the one bragging about your conquests." She barely stopped herself from wincing at the word. "I would've put pettiness past you, but clearly, I'm a poor judge of character."

"You hold me responsible for your expectations of me?" he said with a short, hard laugh devoid of warmth, starkly in contrast with the melodies that had haunted her dreams. "Let's look at the facts, shall we?"

Unwelcome anticipation thrummed in her chest as she wondered at what accusations he might level against her.

"*You* followed me to the balcony. *You* insisted on anonymity. *You* invited me to bed."

He paused in both speech and stride as if for effect. It worked. Her pulse escalated, her throat dried, and something else far more disturbing throbbed in her lower belly.

"*You* have a boyfriend." Another pause. "I'd say the misjudged character here is yours, Princess."

She'd heard her title spoken in admiration, flirtatiousness, and envy, but never had it sounded like an expletive. The image she'd had of him being big, bad, and dangerous magnified. She should be scared, but strangely, despite him being nearly twice her size, she didn't feel any sense of being in physical danger. Not after experiencing the tenderness of his touch, of his lovemaking. However, considering the knowledge in his possession, the damage he could cause surpassed any physical pain he could inflict.

"A costume party gave you the perfect disguise." Disgust permeated every decibel of his delivery.

She reared back. He thought she'd cheated? How low was his opinion of her?

"Was it a dare? Some game you had going on with your princess friends?"

Unprepared for the barrage of accusations, his words slashed into her, sinking in like a double-edged sword. No one had ever spoken to her with such animosity. No one in Umaasie would dare speak to her like this. Which was the point. Kalahari didn't know her, didn't have any allegiance to her or her kingdom.

As far as he was concerned, she might as well come with a few zeroes tattooed on her forehead, because money had to be his motivation. At least, she hoped so. It meant he could be bought.

With a deep breath, she reeled in the pain his words had carved, pulling her mind away from it, focusing on her end game.

"Who sent you?"

He hadn't expected her comeback, she deduced from the flicker of surprise in his eyes. Having eked out what she hoped would lead to an advantage, she pressed on. "Let's not pretend we don't know your real reason for being in Bagumi at the exact time I'm also here."

"And what would that be?"

"To discredit me."

She'd hoped to see his demeanour shift to worry, but if she'd caused him any disquietude, he hid it well.

"You have an awfully high opinion of yourself.

Ignoring his mockery, she voiced her suspicion.

"It's a video, isn't it?"

His gorgeous face took on a look of curiosity. "A video?"

She should have known he wouldn't just own up to it. Perhaps the idea of taunting her held part of the pull for him.

"Of us," she provided, squaring her shoulders but unable to meet his gaze.

God, she could just picture what the tabloids would do with a sex tape of the princess of Umaasie. Worse. What would her mother think?

"If I did have a recording ..." His tone sounded pseudo-contemplative. "How valuable would it be to you?"

"Name your price."

He snorted. "You royals really are a piece of work. Finicky and pernicious. You don't change much from generation to generation."

The edge in his voice, the venom, caught her off-guard. *You royals?*

"Did you at least take the pains to find out who I am?" he spat out. "If you did, you'd discover I don't need money."

His scent wafted around her, snapping her to alertness. Without her realisation, he'd brought the distance between them to one skirting the edge of propriety. Instinct made her step back. He maintained his approach, forcing her to continue her retreat as if in a game of hunter versus hunted.

She gulped, afraid to ask, but she had to. "Then what do you want?"

His face remained unsmiling although amusement now glinted in his eyes. She soon discovered why as she bumped into something, something solid that halted her movement. He'd backed her into a corner. Literally. Her gaze shot up, eyes widening, locking on his unwavering glare. A couple of steps remained between them, but the only way out was past him.

"Stop!" she ordered, shamed to note it sounded nowhere near the intended command. Her spine straightened, announcing her indignation. "If you mean to intimidate me, Mr Asanti, it's not going to work."

"First of all, it's Kalahari or Kal, never Mr Asanti—unless you work for me, which you don't." He reached her, leaned forward, bracing himself with one hand against the wall, his face several inches away. "Secondly, if anyone should be intimidated, it's the ordinary guy who fancies a goddess."

They shouldn't be in such proximity. Though, like her, he'd have had to pass a PCR test before being allowed to meet the king, so they were relatively safe being this close. The heaving of her chest stemmed from an entirely different cause.

As if he knew where her mind had gone, his gaze dropped to her lips. She forced back the urge to lick them as several charged seconds elapsed.

"Someone will walk in any minute," she breathed.

"I can see how that would be a problem for you."

So appealing to his good sense would get her nowhere. She needed to resort to other tactics. She shifted but failed to find any wiggle room. Given his size, there was no way she could push past him.

"Release me," she said, happy to hear the steadiness in her voice.

Her heart sank when he didn't budge.

Inserting more resolve into her tone, she commanded, "Let me go or I'll—"

"Or you'll what?" he interjected on a sneer, his voice several octaves lower, which resonated in her centre. "Scream?"

His lips curled up in a contemptuous smile, his eyes narrowing. "Go ahead, Princess. I dare you."

She blinked. It should come as no surprise that the idea of causing a scene didn't bother him. She had more to lose from such an act.

Looking into his eyes turned out to be a mistake, because the dark orbs caged her will, robbing her of words. She became acutely aware of his scent surrounding her, ushering in vivid memories of his kisses. Under his hot gaze, her insides blossomed like a sunflower to the sun. The thrumming in her core became full-blown arousal.

"I'm getting engaged," she squeaked, though it was as much a caution for him as to herself. She couldn't be found in the arms of another man.

A tremble stole through her. He'd touched her, his palm heating her neck, his thumb skirting the edges of her lips. She should have conjured some strength into her arms and slapped him, but his touch had frozen her limbs. Her heartbeat echoed in her ears, deafening, yet when he whispered, it transmitted to her brain cells unfiltered.

"You're shaking." His fingers dug through her hair, caressing her scalp, causing a deluge of sensations to wash over her.

Without wanting to, she succumbed to the tiniest of moans.

"Does his touch make you tremble? Do you burn for him as you did for me? Or do you think about me while you fuck him?"

She stiffened, inexplicably wounded by his words. "Kalahari ... please don't."

As if the sound of his name on her lips caused him pain, he flinched and tore away from her. The warmth he'd blanketed her in lifted, leaving an undesirable chill in its wake. She realised something, though—she could breathe. She shut her eyes and sucked in a calming lungful of air.

"Good morning, my Princess. Mr Asanti. My name is Tianah Ofori."

Her eyes flew open at the greeting, her gaze encountering a woman she'd met briefly. Her heart continued pounding, heat creeping to her face and neck. Had the other woman heard any of her conversation with Kal? Her impassive face—what could be seen around her nose mask—held no revelations.

"My apologies for keeping you waiting. I had to attend to an emergency situation," she explained, seemingly oblivious to the tension in the room.

"No harm done," Kal said, glancing at the painting. "Her Royal Highness and I have been admiring the artwork."

She swallowed, discreetly passing her tongue over her lips. How could he sound self-assured when she felt so disoriented? More importantly, how could she expect to extract information from him when being near him drove every feminine cell in her body to distraction?

CHAPTER NINE

Kal wanted to punch something—and he would later tonight when he hit the gym. For now, he needed to figure out how to get through the day without losing his sanity. *By God*, if he'd known coming to Bagumi would put her in his path again, he might never have come. Seeing her again had shaken him.

He'd thought their first encounter had been momentous, but today proved everything he'd felt at their first meeting had been child's play. Seeing the face behind the tattoo with minimal make-up and a bold coat of plum on those luscious lips had been earth-shattering enough, but having her to himself—even for a brief fifteen minutes—smelling her, breathing her in, touching her ... seeing desire flare in her eyes, fighting the urge to kiss her ... had nearly unravelled him.

Until she'd tried to bribe him.

It should have cured him of his attraction to her, but he hadn't been able to disengage. He'd yielded to her pull, looked into her eyes, and found himself trapped in their bewitching brown depths.

A car in the next lane honked, the sound yanking him back to the present. Inexorably, his gaze trailed to her.

Edina Dampare.

She sat as far from him as the confines of the limo would allow, focusing on the scenery although nothing out there matched her stunning beauty. Her back, ramrod straight, gave a certain pertness to the rise and fall of her breasts. She was ignoring him, and he found something alluring in the act. Maybe a little perverted, but it confirmed he hadn't misread the signs. Their encounter in the waiting room had rattled her—not just because she thought she had something to fear about him, but because his effect on her was still as potent as it had been that night.

He swore silently. What did it matter? *Taken.* She belonged to someone linked to King Ibrahim, which put her firmly in enemy camp.

"Right," Tianah who'd been tapping and swiping at her mini-tablet, said, drawing him out of his thoughts. "I'm sorry. I didn't mean to be rude, but I had to send an urgent email."

"No offence taken," he assured her.

Edina nodded her acknowledgement with a slight upturn of her lips before returning her attention beyond the car window.

"We're almost there," Tianah announced moments later as they approached an archway entrance to the Bagumi Institute of Research and Cultural Heritage—BIRCH for short.

"What's going on over there?" Edina asked, pointing to a group of people near the gate, some holding placards with various messages on them. "Isn't there a ban on public gatherings?"

"Gatherings are restricted to groups of fifty or less and no more than forty minutes." Tianah huffed. "Appears to be a peace march. They began after Prince Zawadi announced his abdication. Some citizens say the succession rules are outdated. They believe a man shouldn't lose his birth right because he followed his heart."

"Surely, they know the rules weren't created on a whim," Edina said. "It may not favour Prince Zawadi, but it preserves the sanctity of the royal line."

"There are, of course, others who feel as you do, my Princess."

Tianah smiled, but her expression didn't reveal her take on the issue. He didn't offer his opinion either. Kal frowned, surveying the crowd. They were all wearing nose masks. Some even had gloves on. "I don't see any security. Isn't that risky?"

"Nothing serious. Museum guards will move them along if they lurk around too long," Tianah replied.

He studied the group further. There couldn't have been more than thirty people, about a third of whom were female. He also counted five children of varying ages. It seemed tame enough.

The vehicle slowed down, making a cautious approach. Someone noticed the car and pointed, yelling something in Bagumian and drawing the attention of the others. They all turned to look. Some waved. The two ladies waved back. The driver honked a warning as a few attempted to come too close to the car. They passed through without incident, and parked a couple of minutes later.

The entire time it took from the palace to the museum grounds, Edina never looked directly at him. Try as he may, he couldn't seem to take his eyes off her.

As he exited the car, a commotion back at the main entrance caught his attention. The peaceful protest seemed to have turned into an argument between two guys. It escalated fast after one of them threw a punch. The other man returned the favour. Most people in the crowd backed off. A woman who couldn't be more than five-foot-four bravely stepped up, but was shoved aside. It didn't seem to deter her.

Kal glanced around. Where was the palace security Tianah had mentioned? He had to do something before the woman got hurt.

"What is he doing?" Edina said, sprinting towards them, surprisingly agile in her wedge heels.

That propelled him into action. No way would he let her get in the middle of a fight.

He reached the crowd just as the men pushed the woman to the ground. He paused long enough to ensure she wasn't hurt before moving to separate the men.

"Hey, stop!" Edina yelled, still running.

"There's a car coming!" someone shouted.

He turned and realised what he'd missed before. She'd been running towards the street, her singular attention on a little boy chasing after his balloon. The oncoming vehicle blared its horn.

Shit! Releasing the man, he sprinted after her. She got to the child just as he reached the curb and she pulled him aside. Someone grabbed the boy, but Edina lost her footing and slipped.

His heart bottomed out as he watched her fall. Powerlessness wasn't an emotion he'd encountered often in his adult life, but the realisation that he'd never make it to her in time nearly paralysed him. The next few seconds happened so fast, he could only watch.

She rolled to the side, hitting her head against the curb, and went still. The car, which hadn't stopped honking, swerved—thankfully—in the opposite direction and went over the curb on the reverse side.

Propelled back into motion, he reached her and knelt beside her. Someone came to squat on the other side. He raised his gaze briefly and found Tianah's worried face.

"Is she unconscious?" she asked.

He cupped Edina's cheek, and she groaned, opening her eyes. Relief washed over him, and he released a breath he'd inadvertently been holding.

"My Princess, thank God!" Tianah exclaimed. "The king will not be happy about this."

His jaw tightened at the remark, but he focused on the more important issue.

"Are you okay? Do you feel any pain?"

She shook her head, then winced as she tried to move again. "My ankle. I may have twisted it."

He checked it. "Feels a little tender, but no broken bones. How's your head?"

"Fine. I didn't hit it hard."

She tried to stand.

"Don't move."

"The boy—"

"He's fine," he said. "Don't try to stand."

Slipping his arm around her, he helped her to sit up. Presently, he shifted his focus to events around them. Museum security had finally arrived. The fight had been broken, although that was probably a result of Edina risking her life to save someone's child. The boy, now safely in his mother's arms, didn't appear worse for wear.

Although the security seemed to be doing a good job keeping the crowd at bay, the number of onlookers were increasing with many smartphones out.

"We need to get her inside," he said to Tianah.

She nodded, also taking in the scene. "We've prepared an office for her inside. We can use the private entrance."

His gaze returned to Edina. Aside from the sprained ankle, a bruise on her forehead, and slightly dishevelled hair, she appeared fine.

"You shouldn't put pressure on the foot. Not before a doctor has checked you out."

"He's right, my Princess," Tianah said.

Edina nodded. With her assent, he slipped his other hand underneath her legs and lifted her into his arms.

"Lead the way."

***

Edina had held her breath the moment she'd turned and seen the little boy chasing after his balloon oblivious to the dangers of his actions. The fall had knocked the wind out of her. Then Kal had picked her up, and she forgot about breathing altogether.

As they entered the building via the private entrance Tianah had mentioned, she held on to him, trying not to show how much she liked being in his arms again, feeling his heartbeat against her ribs, his scent permeating her senses. It took all her willpower to keep from resting her head on his chest.

When they reached the office, he laid her down on a sofa. She moaned in reflex at the sudden sense of cold and abandonment of not being in his arms.

Tianah came to her side, brows creased in arcs of concern. "Are you in a lot of pain?"

She shook her head, but didn't attempt sitting up. "I'm fine, really. I just need a minute. I'll take a painkiller if I need it."

"I've called the medics on duty, so they can check you as a precaution." She thrust an icepack and a tub of hand sanitiser in front of her. "Use this in the meantime."

She nodded, applying the sanitiser before taking the icepack and placing it on the side of her head. She sighed at the soothing sensation brought on by the cold. She hadn't failed to notice Kal had retreated to the side-lines. Though he'd taken off his mask, she couldn't see his face as the window behind cast him in a silhouette. What was he doing all the way over there? *Social distancing, duh.* Was she nuts for wanting him to be the one fussing over her?

"You're one brave woman," Tianah started, but was interrupted by her phone ringing. She paused to check the screen. "I knew he'd call."

Whoever 'he' was, Tianah looked as if she'd rather avoid the impending conversation.

"I'll take this outside." She swiped the phone screen on her way out. "Hello. Yes, my Prince."

The moment Tianah left the room, tension rose. Her gaze returned to Kal. Despite her inability to see his face properly, she felt his stare. Her heartbeat escalated, and a warm feeling pooled in her belly. Geez, the man must ooze pheromones in droves, because all she could think about was being in his arms again.

She swallowed, giving herself a mental shake. She couldn't afford to let him see how much his proximity affected her. Or anything he could exploit against her.

She cleared her throat. "Are you just going to stand there like a bodyguard?"

He inhaled audibly, stepping away from the window.

"Do you do this sort of thing often?" he asked, in lieu of an answer to her question.

"What sort of thing?"

"Almost get yourself killed." His voice was a low growl of impatience.

She blinked, taken aback.

"What you did was dangerous," he continued. "Brave, but dangerous."

"What choice did I have? The boy was running into the road, and everybody's attention was on the fight."

"Had anything gone wrong, you could have endangered both you *and* the child."

Anger? Really? Was he kidding her right now? What did he have to be annoyed about? She was the one who'd fallen and bumped her head and almost got run over by a car.

"Nothing went wrong, and I saved the boy, in case you missed that part." Emotion gave her voice a sharp edge, but she didn't care. "The least you could do is be nice."

He laughed—a throaty, yet mirthless sound. "You'll soon discover, Princess, I'm not in the business of being nice. Unless you have training in what you did, you got lucky."

"You know nothing about me. Don't be deceived by the fact that I'm a woman."

"A princess," he emphasised.

"You have no idea the skills I'm required to have, the lessons I've had to undertake my whole life."

His eyes narrowed, his face briefly contorting with an expression she couldn't decipher. "Believe me, I do."

She frowned. "How could you? You grew up without the entanglements of royalty, free to do anything you wanted with your time."

He shook his head.

"I didn't." Seconds ticked by as she waited for him to elaborate. "My mother used to be a servant girl who was treated unfairly by her employer. When she had me, she vowed I'd never grow up feeling like I didn't measure up to anyone. Not even a prince. So I had the misfortune of my own set of rules, restrictions, and training."

"Like dancing," she said.

He nodded.

"And sports, language, music. You name it." His eyes gained a faraway look as he released a short laugh. "We didn't have money, so she found creative ways to get me lessons."

Her brows hooked up. "Like what?"

"Working at a polo club in exchange for horse riding and polo sessions, my mother sewing free uniforms for the coach's kids so he'd teach me boxing, housekeeping without pay in exchange for her boss settling my elementary school fees."

Despite her experience with him, she got the sense he wasn't a chatty person. It solidified the significance of this revelation. She stared at him for a long moment, acknowledging something she hadn't given a second thought when they'd met. Everything about him seemed deliberate. From his choice of designer shoes and suit to his comportment and diction. He even wore his hair exactly as she remembered, styled as though each short spongy loc had been precisely placed. What was his full story? Why did he seem to harbour so much anger? Why did she even care?

A sudden pain shot through her head, making her wince. She closed her eyes for a second, resting her head back on the chair.

"What is it?"

He sounded close. She reopened her eyes and found him standing in front of her. The concern in his gaze staggered her, belying his previous declaration. He cared. The revelation coupled with his nearness did things to her body she didn't want to think about, things that shouldn't coexist with pain.

He shook his head. "You must be trying to get me in trouble."

She blinked, frowning. "What?"

"You keep looking at me like that, Princess, and I'm going to have to kiss you."

Gasping, she cast her gaze aside. She needed to come up with a mantra to stop herself from remembering, from yearning ... especially in his presence.

"Smart woman," he muttered before stepping back.

She refused to dwell on the sense of rejection his retreat caused. Instead, she searched her mind for an appropriate line of conversation. Thankfully, the door opened, and Tianah swept in, saving her the trouble.

CHAPTER TEN

Seven in the evening found Kal at the Olympic Training Centre, which had been built for Prince Zareb's preparation towards the Olympics. It had been closed to the public, but palace guests were still allowed its use. He'd followed the necessary protocols to ensure he could. He had no company, which suited him well. He needed to let off some steam, and he preferred to do it without an audience.

After his warm-up, he went for the speed bags, his poison of choice today because they demanded focus, speed, and control—all things he needed to bring his emotions in check. Eyeing the speed bag like a fighter would an opponent, he landed a series of alternating punches with his fists and elbows just to keep things interesting. After twenty minutes of that, he vented his vexation on a punching bag. He would have gone for weights next if he'd thought it would help.

By now, he'd accepted nothing could blot out the image of Edina nearly getting run over by a car. It had all but stopped his heart. Fear wasn't the only thing he'd felt today. He'd been proud of her— of her instinct and precision, her selflessness.

There'd also been anger—at her for endangering herself, and at himself for giving a damn.

His mind dredged back her accusation of him filming their affair, of trying to use it to tarnish her image.

With a frustrated growl, he returned to the speed bag, attacking it with greater power and speed in hopes of forcing his mind to focus more on his swinging force and rhythmic accents.

It proved ineffective. He could still see her face in his mind, still smell her. His heart congealed into lead when he remembered she belonged to someone else.

He'd never been given to jealousy, but thinking of her with Zik made him want to punch the daylights out of the guy.

He reminded him of his reasons for being in Bagumi and renewed his resolve.

He'd made another important decision. He wanted Edina, and he wouldn't be deterred by her relationship. He'd woo her away from the prince— not because he had anything against the guy. Zik could have any woman he wanted, but Edina was it for Kal. No other woman had affected him like her.

"Looks like you have a few issues to work out."

The unexpected remark stole Kal's focus, and he stopped punching the bag to face Prince Zareb.

"You can say that." Zareb didn't appear to be a talker, but just to be sure he didn't delve into details, Kal nodded towards his full fencing outfit. "I read you've stopped competing."

"I have, but I coach. At least, I'll resume when things return to normal, so I still have to train daily."

Kal silently applauded the dedication. He had a sense if they'd grown up together, he might have gotten along well with Zareb.

He then caught himself. Considering the path he'd chosen, he didn't have any business noticing admirable familial qualities in any of the Saenes.

"You should try fencing," Zareb suggested with a glance towards the speed bag. "I have a few minutes to spare. I can give you a quick lesson."

"I know the basics." Kal conceded a brief lift of one corner of his lips at Zareb's raised eyebrows. "My mother thought I needed to learn a refined sport."

"A wise woman."

Except in her love for King Ibrahim.

"She was." The anticipated awkward moment ensued—when the other party realised the use of past tense, usually followed by words of apology as if they had something to do with the death. "She passed on recently."

"I'm sorry to hear that." Oddly enough, the guy seemed genuinely sympathetic. "Perhaps if your schedule allows, you'll agree to a match with me in her honour?"

"I'll keep that in mind."

There would, of course, be no match. After the events of the next few days, the prince would withdraw his invitation. He'd probably want to run his sword through Kal's heart instead.

***

Edina didn't believe in avoidance tactics, but today, she fully intended to play ostrich. After the emotional overload upon seeing Kal again, she didn't have the energy to field any more darts from his charm. Worse, her own mind seemed bent on conspiring against her. She'd endured a sleepless night having nothing to do with the mild headache and few bruises she'd sustained from her heroics.

Added to the partial lockdown in effect, she decided to work from her guest suite. By noon, fatigue had set in.

Her mind needed no other excuse to drift to the topic of Kal, and her body began to tingle all over. Seeing him again, finding herself in his arms, had disoriented her. How could he still make her weak in the knees with just a look?

Thankfully, all the images and posts from yesterday she'd seen on social media so far had been tasteful, most calling her a hero and him a knight in shining armour. The images of her being carried by him had thumping-heart emojis and GIFs of people swooning accompanying each comment.

Her phone buzzed, interrupting her thoughts. She answered without checking the caller ID. Her best friend's familiar voice drifted across the line. Even with the greeting, she sensed something amiss.

"What's wrong, Jamila?"

"Zoraya ruffling feathers again."

She sighed. "What's my infamous cousin done this time?"

"Trying to get support for a Chinese mining conglomerate to construct and manage our mines."

A chuckle followed. "Your brother needs to put her on a short leash."

"He'd like to, I'm sure, but she's family."

"Family doesn't try to drug other members and leave them at the mercy of a group of uncouth male friends."

She couldn't help flinching at the comment. Spiking Edina's drink at a party had been her cousin's meanest act by far in her desire to steal the title of Princess of the Crown. It had taken Edina a long time to get past the betrayal. She didn't want to think about it now.

"That was in university," she said.

"Making her old enough to know exactly what she was doing."

"It's in the past. Can we drop it?"

"Yes, please. That's not even why I called." Jamila's voice lowered as she continued. "Who's that tall glass of chocolate mousse in the photos with you, because I know that's not your soon-to-be fiancé."

"Oh, God, has my mother seen them?"

"Yes, and she thinks this will ginger Nana Siriboe II to rush and stake his claim on you."

She grimaced.

"Who is he? Is he single?"

Edina took in a breath. "It's him."

"Who?"

"The Warrior."

"No. Way!" Jamila gasped. "Wait. What's he doing in Bagumi?"

"Exactly!"

She narrated the events of the past twenty-four hours.

"You really think he may have recorded you?"

"If not, then what kind of coincidence is this?"

"Why wait so long, though? It's been almost nine months."

"I don't know. The pandemic may have thwarted his plans before now."

"Could Zoraya be behind it?"

A chill ran up her spine, chasing out her initial instinct to debunk the idea. It made sense. Her cousin had everything to gain from Edina's disgrace. She had no doubt Zoraya would capitalise on her shame and try to convince her brother to strip her of the title. She couldn't let it happen.

"You need to find out for sure if he has a video or photos," Jamila continued.

"How?"

"Seduction worked once."

"No." She rejected the suggestion immediately. "That's what got me in hot waters to begin with."

"Do you have a better idea?"

She didn't. Her research on him yesterday had left her with a mix of awe and trepidation. He'd told her he was a financier, but many articles referred to him as a modern-day corporate raider. He was an angel investor in many promising business ideas, but his speciality or love lay in acquiring failing companies and disintegrating them. He kept the most profitable portions in his portfolio and sold the rest for profit.

Although traditional methods of hostile takeovers were decreasing in popularity and effectiveness, it appeared Kalahari had a knack for finding creative ways of achieving his aims. Some called him ruthless; others saw him as an artist. Speculation surrounded his methods, but it seemed even a rumour of his interest in a company could affect the price of its stock. Either way, she couldn't compete with the man she'd learnt about in her research. Not without careful planning. That required time, of which she didn't have the luxury.

Reluctantly, she reconsidered her friend's proposal. It would be an easy way to get close enough to him. Her mind drifted back to their night together. Seducing Kal would be like playing with fire. Could she do it without getting burnt?

CHAPTER ELEVEN

Edina thought it a shame the palace flower gardens weren't open to the public. Though standing amid the gorgeous blooms of delicate whites, rich yellows, shocking oranges, and so many other vibrant colours, she couldn't help being happy to enjoy this moment without an audience.

A butterfly flitted in front of her. She smiled, watching its carefree movements and musing about the stark difference between their respective lives. The insect, free and unencumbered; she, following a defined path of expectations. Find a husband. Produce an heir. Become queen. She sighed. It seemed her whole existence was one giant wait to start living.

Except for that one night when she'd truly existed in the moment, when a glance across a room had zeroed in on the most beautiful man she'd ever laid eyes on, in whose arms she'd fully blossomed from girl to woman. Those few hours of her life had turned her world on its axis—a moment of pleasure, which could now cost her everything.

Since talking to Jamila, she'd been strategizing ... or trying to. It didn't help that each time she closed her eyes, her mind fetched other thoughts ... specifically of Kal—like in the waiting room the other day ... the way his eyes had devoured her, the feel of his thumb on her lips, his warm breath on her face, his voice humming through her like the tune of the pied piper, luring her with its magic.

A gentle breeze caressed her face, carrying along floral scents of various tropical blooms. Out here, the cares she carried seemed to evaporate. She closed her eyes and inhaled deeply, emptying her mind.

'Do you burn for him as you did for me?'

Her eyes flew open. For a second, she expected to find Kal standing next to her. Thankfully, her solitude hadn't been encroached upon. She forced his voice out of her head, annoyed at the invasion instigated by her own mind. Quickening her pace, she focused on putting one foot in front of the other, counting her steps. Engaging her mind with the mundane task kept her from succumbing to unwanted thoughts.

She'd nearly hit a hundred when she stopped abruptly. She'd gone beyond the main garden and now found herself surrounded by a cluster of trees providing moist ground for jewel-weed to flourish. The palace wasn't far, but the trees made it barely visible from her vantage point. She should probably return now, especially since she'd ventured out on her own. However, something in her resisted the idea, drawn in by the serenity of her surroundings. A few metres ahead, she spotted a wooden bench and went over to sit.

She lost track of time as she began humming various tunes.

"Hiding from someone?"

Damn that raspy voice. Even communion with nature couldn't rid her mind of it.

Wait a second. It sounded too real, too potent to be in her head. Crunching footsteps confirmed her suspicion.

She turned.

Kal.

Her heart thumped as her eyes raked over his broad torso which tapered into tight abs and lean hips. He slipped his hands into his trouser pockets, drawing her attention to his fly.

"Liking what you see?"

Crap! She yanked her gaze up, met his electric grey eyes. His lips curved in a slow, sexy smile.

She swallowed. "I was looking for some privacy. You're invading."

"I saw you wondering off all alone."

"And you thought I needed a chaperone?"

"I thought you might like some company." He leaned against one tree. "Would you like me to leave?"

She stood. "No need. I'll find another spot."

As she walked past him, his hand closed around her wrist, his grip loose enough for her to rescue her arm. She didn't. Maybe because the contact left her unprepared, or she'd secretly wished for it, or perhaps because it felt so good, she wanted to absorb a little more of it before leaving.

Her lips parted as her brain attempted to find something to say. She looked into his eyes, and any potential words disintegrated into the cool late Bagumian afternoon air.

"Stay," he said.

Why did his voice always give her tingles? He may have tugged her; she might have moved of her own volition, succumbing to the familiar pull only he had over her. The space between them shrank.

"Why?" her suddenly husky voice asked.

"Do you need a reason?"

"Yes."

She nearly flinched. Had she really said that? Thank goodness he wasn't one of her suitors, since her brain and lungs seemed to operate at suboptimal levels in his company.

"How about because you want to?" he provided, his tone a decibel lower. Her hormones had never been happier. "You don't really want to run away from me, do you?"

"I should," she replied. "You're a dangerous man."

His look hardened, and he released her. "You think I'll hurt you?"

She conceded a brief smile, shaking her head. "There are worse ways to harm a person than the physical."

The hard edges around his features softened as his look turned pensive. "Wise words, Princess."

"Are you averse to addressing me by name?"

"No, but I need to remind myself who you are."

She frowned. "I'm the same person you met."

"No, you're not." His eyes bore into hers, his gaze fraught with accusation.

Guilt niggled at her. She'd been dishonest by omission, but the anonymity had bolstered her. If only she'd known how pointless it would be. Sadly, now, she desired more than anything to hear him speak her name. Would it sound like a caress to her senses?

She looked away, pretending to admire the foliage around them. Hopefully, her thoughts hadn't been laid bare through the windows of her eyes. She'd made one mistake with him already. She didn't need another.

"You may look exactly like her," he continued. "You're every bit as tempting, but the woman I met was fearless and passionate. You're restraining her, limiting her."

Her breath quickened. Words swirled in her head, words that would agree with him, confess how much she wanted to be liberated from her obligations, free to want whomever she pleased, free to want him.

How did she explain why she had to repress the desires he'd awakened in her? Without political obligations, he had the liberty to make his own rules. He'd never appreciate any system where one didn't have those freedoms.

"You're different, too," she said.

He'd been so open to her before, allowing himself to be vulnerable. The man standing before her now was reticent.

He shrugged without responding. Instead, he asked, "Do you love him?"

***

Kal's breath halted as she turned her bottomless honey eyes back on him. He didn't know how he managed to keep standing with his hands in his pockets—the picture of nonchalance—because he felt certain the earth had shifted underneath his feet.

He should no longer be surprised by her effect on him, but for some reason, he continued to question his sanity. She was one of *them*, for crying out loud. His desire for her should have waned the moment he'd learnt her identity. Yet, he found himself unable to accomplish the simple task of averting his gaze.

The soft fabric of her long-flowing dress paid homage to every curve of her delectable body—to his immense pleasure and frustration.

He returned his attention to her face. A look he couldn't decipher filled her captivating, almond-shaped eyes. Disapproval? He didn't blame her. He asked himself the same question that must be on her mind. Why did he care whether or not she loved her future husband?

"There's something I should tell you, Kal," she said. "I'm not dating Zik."

He blinked. Several seconds ticked by while he tried to gather his thoughts. He knew he hadn't misheard before. Meaning she'd been deliberately dishonest with him. Again.

"Say something," she pleaded.

"You lied to me. Is that your thing?" His voice came out harsh. "You told me you were getting engaged."

"I am. Just not to him."

"Then my question remains valid."

"Marriage has nothing to do with love."

For several seconds, he watched her, noted her resolute stance, shoulders drawn. He had a feeling she didn't believe her own words. He didn't challenge her, though. A part of him applauded her for not trying to sell him some misguided fairy tale. If she didn't have wool over her eyes, then she was smarter than most. More than he could say for Mamaa.

"What's in it for you, then?"

"He's a man of noble birth and upbringing. We'd make a good match."

"Sounds like something your parents said to convince you."

She gave a resigned sigh, then turned sideways. His gaze lingered on the perky rise of her bosom, narrowing into a slim waist accentuated by a chain belt.

"I'm not at liberty to marry just anyone," she said.

He knew what she really meant. *He* didn't qualify. Would she change her mind if she knew King Ibrahim was his biological father? That would tick at least one of the boxes. A part of him wanted to tell her, but he shook off the urge. His trust had to be earned, and she hadn't. She'd been insincere with him twice. More importantly, she had to want him for himself and nothing else.

"I grew up with one job," she said. "To produce an heir to the throne and maintain the sanctity of the royal lineage. I was raised with the expectation of simply marrying well. I went to the right schools, ensuring my circle of friends comprised of suitable men. Titled or noble men, especially ones with wealth and connections that could benefit the country."

He quirked a brow. "What's your boyfriend bringing to the table?"

"Renewable energy."

He whistled.

She glanced at him, folding her arms beneath her breasts. "He's not my boyfriend. We've only met once two years ago. His father is acquainted with my mum."

Tension eased around his insides. He'd been suffocating since she'd told him about her impending engagement. He didn't know why she'd chosen to confide in him, but he sensed this wasn't a conversation she'd had with many people, if anyone. Warmth unfurled in his chest at the thought of being chosen by her.

Her eyes held a melancholic resolve, and it became clear to him—the reason she'd accused him of recording their affair. A relationship with her wouldn't be about just the two people involved. Any blemish to her image could have huge consequences.

Just like in business. A scandal involving a CEO could tank the value of the company's shares, sometimes irreparably. She couldn't trust anyone, which made everyone the enemy. What a burden for a person to carry. At least, he knew the identity of his foe.

"What if no children ensue from your marriage?" he asked.

"I dare not think of the possibility."

"Avoidance doesn't take away the consequences."

He saw hesitation in her posture.

"Dare to go there," he pressed. "Tell me."

After a moment, she sighed. "Umaasie is a diarchy."

"Two monarchs?"

"The king and queen co-reign. Some matters are the purview of the queen's court." She paused. "Before you ask, the king's wife is just his consort. The queen is a female member of the king's bloodline. Currently, that's my mother."

She didn't say more, but she didn't have to.

"Someday, you'll be queen."

She nodded.

"If my marriage produces no heirs, I'd have to give up my position as Princess of the Crown to my cousin. The throne moves from my line to hers. She's bad news." She gave an embarrassed laugh. "I don't know why I'm telling you all this."

"Perhaps for the same reason I can't stay away from you."

Their eyes held. It supercharged his heart. If he didn't leave, he'd close the distance between them, pull her into his arms, and kiss her worries away. He wouldn't, though.

A change had occurred within him, one so subtle, he couldn't pinpoint when it happened. It was no longer just about him and what he wanted. She might be one of them, but he cared what happened to her.

He still meant to woo her, though. After what she'd just told him, however, he knew he had to be subtle, win her heart before she realised what he was doing.

It meant showing an act of good faith.

"I didn't record us."

Her brows creased, doubt flashing in her eyes. "You didn't?"

"I'm not one of your enemies."

"Then what are you doing in Bagumi?"

"I have personal business here."

"The museum project," she stated.

"Among other things."

As if he'd uttered some magic word, relief spread over her face. The next thing he knew, she was in his arms, embracing him. Her softness pressed against him, her warmth engulfing him, her scent ... By God, her scent. His arms wrapped around her as though by design.

"Thank you," she whispered.

She hadn't pulled away yet. The rise and fall of her chest intensified. Was she crying? Before he could decide what to do about it, he became aware of her fingers at his nape. They moved against his skin, softly. She was rubbing his neck.

Of their own volition, his hands responded with caresses at her back. He tilted his head, grazing her temple with his lips. He shouldn't be doing this. He needed to slow down and not scare her away. But her scent had intoxicated him, paralysed his good sense.

"You fit perfectly in my arms, *ma chérie*, like you're meant for me."

She stiffened as if realising just then what was happening. She pulled back, and he loosened his hold without releasing her. The heat of their embrace continued to burn, hot and all-consuming.

She stared into his eyes, her breathing hiked, body trembling against his. Her lips parted, beckoning.

He didn't know where he garnered the strength, but he managed to call up enough of it to relinquish his hold. He turned to leave.

He'd taken several steps when she called after him. "I knew it."

He stopped.

"Deep down, you're one of the good guys."

"In another lifetime, perhaps, but in this one? I'm not a good guy."

"Then why didn't you kiss me?"

She didn't just—

He swore, turned. She stood there, exactly where he'd left her, every captivating curve and dip on display as a breeze moulded the dress around her body. The hunger in her eyes nearly undid him. He inhaled, mentally digging in his heels.

She swallowed, licked her lips, and his resolve snapped. Passion blinded him. In a flash, he closed the distance between them, jerked her into his arms. The impact pushed her breath out in a puff. His mouth descended on hers, his tongue taking full advantage of her parted lips.

She took him in, her body going pliant as she moaned and whimpered, firing his desire. Her hands gripped him, and he half-expected her to push him away. Instead, she clutched fistfuls of his shirt, her fingernails digging into his sides. He groaned. For over half a year, he'd been thinking about this, yearning for her. She tasted as good as he remembered. Better.

His every instinct begged him to lift her dress and rip her panties off, take her right here in the open air, surrounded by the music of nature. If he didn't stop now, he might end up alienating her instead. Offending the king's guest would probably get him thrown out of the kingdom before he could gain access to the information he needed. He couldn't have that.

He yanked her away from him, trying to bring his breathing under control. The exhilaration in her eyes made him want to pull her back and claim her as he'd done the night of the ball.

"Never dare me like that again, because the next time we kiss, I'll be making love with you, and I won't care whether you have a boyfriend."

"This was just—" She shook her head, catching her breath. "There won't be a next time."

After the way she'd kissed him?

"I promise you, Honey Eyes, there will be."

With that, he turned and walked away before he changed his mind.

Chapter Twelve

A knock came on his door on Friday morning, drawing Kal from his laptop. He frowned, checking the time. Who the hell would visit him at six in the morning? Personally, he could think of only one person he wanted to see at his doorstep. He'd barely seen her since the other day in the woods, though she'd never wandered far from his mind.

Over the past couple of days, he'd kept a busy schedule, meeting with the stakeholders regarding the funding for the restoration exercise. A draft agreement had been developed, which he'd forwarded to the foundation's legal counsel for review.

He'd also been gathering information and found exactly what he needed to set Plan A into motion. He just had to wait for the right time to make his move. As insurance, Shaka was digging up dirt on each member of the family. He'd require it, since they were unlikely to accept defeat lying down.

As he threw on a T-shirt, the tap-tap-tap sounded again—insistent without being impatient.

"Just a minute," he called out, hibernating his laptop and putting away any documents that might raise questions.

As a precaution, he sent a message to Shaka who had men close by to take action if anything went wrong. He might have to consider moving out of the palace before the end of his stay.

He yanked the door open, rearing back as his gaze encountered the visitor.

"King Ibrahim!"

Belatedly, he remembered to bow. His brows drew together at the absence of the monarch's security detail or his Chief of Staff. He supposed the man didn't need round the clock protection in his own castle.

"I need a private word."

"Of course."

He stepped back and held the door open. As the king entered, Kal cast a glance around, expecting to spot a bodyguard lurking just out of sight. He didn't. Shutting the door, he turned to face Ibrahim, unsure whether the man expected some additional act of deference. He reckoned these were his quarters, making the king a mere guest. He didn't get to demand more than the initial bow.

For several seconds, the older man stood in the middle of the room, his gaze surveying Kal as if searching for something. Kal quirked a brow. What could be so important to warrant this visit? Had the king gotten an inkling of his real purpose in Bagumi? If so, wouldn't Prince Zareb be there with a dozen men at hand to arrest him?

"How may I help you, Your Majesty?"

"Are you mine?"

His back stiffened, though he tried not to show his surprise. His heart hammered against his ribcage at the unexpected question.

Brows creased, he pretended to misunderstand the question. "Yours?"

"Are you my son?"

He could have said yes, shortened the conversation and gone for the kill, but something made him hesitate, made him want to hold on to his anonymity for a little longer. In his heart, he'd always be the son of Xavier Dubane. For the first time, he allowed a thought he'd forbidden himself to entertain. Would *he* approve?

He shoved the thought aside. As much as he loved the man who'd had a short five years to raise him and show him what a father's love ought to be, it wasn't enough to cure him of his need to avenge his mother.

"What makes you think I am?"

"You're Yara's son. You're the right age." With a sigh, the king turned and crossed the breadth of the room, putting more distance between them. "The other day at breakfast, you looked every bit like one of my children."

Anger flared, pumping through his veins. "So now I'm good enough to claim as yours? You rejected her and her child, and now that I'm a man of my own means, it's no longer shameful to think of me as your son?"

"You're angry, I understand—"

"Do not patronise me, old man."

The steel in his voice seemed to take the king aback. While he felt no remorse for it, he reined in his emotions, knowing they'd serve more to his detriment.

"I never knew Yara was pregnant."

"Let's pretend I believe you. Would you have done differently?"

"You have to understand—"

"So that's a no."

The older man continued, ignoring the interruption. "I was a young king ruffling a lot of feathers with controversial reforms. Some factions called for my blood. If anyone found out about Yara and me ... I tried to shield her from that. When she left, I accepted the reasons she gave and didn't try to find her."

"Liar," he spat out. "What you are is a selfish man, a man who used his position to coerce a woman way too young and innocent to resist his power. A pregnant staff member would have threatened that power, so you had her exiled from her home."

Ibrahim raised his hand in a conciliatory gesture. "You're right. I was selfish in that I loved your mother and didn't want to live without her."

"Seems you've done just fine without her for the past thirty-two years. You even had six more children in that time."

He stood unmoving, anger still clawing through him, but interlaced with unexpected vacillation. He'd prepared for denial, blame, arrogance. In front of him, however, he saw a man, emotions unmasked as if it was the first time he'd had a chance to talk about this. An act, or real?

Ibrahim turned away. Kal couldn't help suspecting the man needed a moment to gather composure.

"I had reason to believe your mother had someone else, someone who could offer her what I couldn't."

He scoffed. "One minute, you say you loved her. The next, you call her a whore."

The king whipped around. "Don't put words in my mouth, Kalahari. I did love Yara, and I won't have you or anyone question it."

"And *I* won't have you stand there and insult her memory. Not after the way she—" He stopped abruptly, his heart clenching, throat tightening. He sucked in a breath, his hands folding into fists as though he needed to physically hold in the outburst.

The king raised his brows "How? How did she die?"

"We're not having this conversation, so if you've got nothing further to say, I'd like to get back to work."

Ibrahim sighed in a manner that reminded Kal of Xavier's immeasurable patience with him as a hot-headed teen angry with the whole world. Once again, he wondered what Shaka's father would have thought about this mission, but pushed it out of his mind.

"Contrary to what you've been led to believe, Kalahari, I didn't abandon you. I know you don't need me, but if you're my son, I'd like to acknowledge you."

"To what end?"

"To bestow you with the legitimacy of being my son."

"There's nothing you can offer me that I don't already have."

"Surely, there has to be something, or we wouldn't be having this conversation."

His heart thumped, and he fought to control his breathing. He hadn't meant for his identity to be revealed this early in the game. He also hadn't banked on the king suspecting it. This changed everything.

Edina's words filled his mind. *Titled or noble men.*

If that was what she wanted, then he'd give it to her.

He met the king's gaze squarely and went for the ultimate. "I want my birth right. Succession to the throne."

The other man stiffened for a second although he didn't appear shocked by the request.

"Since Yara and I were never married, you'll be considered illegitimate, and therefore, not eligible to ascend to the throne. The rules of the land allow a king to marry his child's mother in order to legitimise their children after the fact, but—"

"There's one exception to that rule, isn't there?" he countered, glad he'd done his homework. "Where an act of nature prevents a possible marriage, if intent can be proven, then the king and king makers have the right of legitimising a child born out of wedlock even without marriage."

The king's look indicated he hadn't expected Kal to know this obscure piece of information.

"How would you prove intent?"

He walked over to his briefcase and retrieved the ring, slipping it on his left pinkie finger. He took a moment to compose himself, knowing the next few minutes could go terribly wrong. He turned, holding out his hand.

Time seemed to stall as the king stared at the ring traditionally given to the first son of each consort.

"I had it checked out, just to be sure it was genuine. It is," he said. "Per their birth rights, Princes Zawadi and Azikiwe have identical rings."

When the king remained silent, Kal spoke again. "The way I see it, Your Majesty, you have two options. Either honour the intent of this ring, or acknowledge the lengths to which you were willing to go to deceive my mother."

The older man's shoulders slumped with the sigh he released. "It's not that simple. There are other conditions necessary for that rule to take effect. You'll need to present your case before the king makers. Even so, as long as I have legitimate heirs, you'll be placed at the end of the line."

Enough to shake the foundations of his family and hang him. Enough to win Edina.

"Works for me." A beat passed. "What next?"

"We'll need incontestable proof of your paternity."

***

As soon as the king left, Kal sent a text message to Shaka.

'Video call. Five minutes'

This was a conversation best had face-to-face. Since they couldn't do it in person, a video chat would have to suffice. The response to his text came almost immediately.

'Already on'

He moved to sit at the desk and dialled before propping the phone against his open laptop. When his brother picked up, he waited a few seconds for the video to load. Unsurprisingly, Shaka was already dressed for the day. Due to the heavy rush hour traffic in Accra, they both made it a point to get out of the house before six. With the one-hour time difference between Darusa and Accra, they had barely ten minutes to talk.

"How soon can you get to Bagumi?"

Shaka smiled as though he'd been expecting this question. "I have a plane on standby. What do you need?"

"A witness." At Shaka's frown, he explained, "Paternity test."

"Things are going that well?"

"Too smoothly." He ran through the king's visit. "He appears to be happy about this. It doesn't make sense."

"You're a world-acclaimed businessman with billion-dollar corporations in several nations across the globe. I doubt there's anyone in the world who'd be reluctant to claim you as his son."

"Thanks for the support. I don't trust him, and I can't figure out his game plan. That worries me."

"Could you have misjudged the man? He may have made a rash decision in his youth. Maybe age has changed him. Know any billionaires who started out as hot-headed teens?"

The reference to his youth made him chuckle, which he suspected had been his brother's intention. He stuck to his guns. "It will take more to convince me."

"What about your princess?"

Something happened in his chest when Shaka mentioned Edina—a quickening of pace, a lightness, a sensation as though his heart had expanded to fit his entire torso.

He frowned, making sure it translated into his tone. "What about her?"

"Just ensuring she isn't distracting you. You need to be focused."

"I'm focused."

The fact that his response came out clipped said it all. Normally, he wouldn't pay any attention to such a comment, but Shaka had a way of stating things in an all-knowing tone that got to him more often than he'd willingly admit.

"Good." Shaka still had the older-brother tone in his voice, buttressed by a matching look. "And Kal?"

"What?"

"If there's any chance you actually like the woman, don't hurt her."

Despite his mood, the comment wheedled a chuckle out of him. "This coming from a guy who's left more than a few broken hearts on every continent?"

"Apples and oranges, brother."

He shook his head, having no interest in pursuing this line of conversation. His mind buzzed with things that needed to be done.

"Sorry, brother, but I have to go."

Shaka nodded. "To answer your question, I can set off by dinner time provided I get all the clearances."

"I'll talk to the king and update you."

With that, he ended the session.

CHAPTER THIRTEEN

"Fascinating."

Edina couldn't keep the awe from her voice while studying the 3D images projected on the wall. Together with a small team of local and visiting scientists, the authenticity of several shards of ceramics had been confirmed. Modern software solutions had made the process much simpler and faster than it had been when she'd been doing her master's in Museum Studies.

The team was still working on a collection of brass instruments which would shed more light on the lifestyle and warfare of an ancient Bagumian tribe of warriors believed to be the ancestors of the royal family.

Next, they'd attempt to identify the original forms of all the broken pieces and digitally reconstruct them. This would help create replicas for sale at the planned exhibition next year.

She continued staring at the intricate designs on the teapot and cups still rotating in front of them. "It's amazing how such tiny objects can reveal an entire legacy."

"Indeed, Your Royal Highness," the museum's curator, Mrs Sauda, commented. "The restoration exercise will be time-consuming and expensive.

We're excited to have Asanti Foundation sponsoring the exercise."

The mention of Kal's organisation conjured a flush of unwarranted excitement. Her best efforts at ignoring it proved futile. She hadn't seen much of him since their kiss in the woods. She'd believed him when he'd assured her he had no recording of them. She'd heard of the endless meetings that took up his days and confirmed his personal business interests in Bagumi. The knowledge had caused a flood of relief and quashed the remnants of her reservations.

"Did you know he's committed to matching any funds we raise at the end of every year for the next decade?"

She hadn't known. "Really?"

"Handsome and generous," Mrs Sauda said with a girlish giggle despite being over fifty.

The last comment set her mind rolling, toying with the idea of pitching Umaasie to him. An investment from his company could do wonders for the economy of a tiny nation like hers.

Yet, the pep in her heartbeat at the notion of hosting him in her home signalled danger.

She should discard the idea. She didn't need any more exposure to him than required during the time they were both in Bagumi. It would be in her own interest to avoid him as much as possible until he left. Once the necessary formalities had been dealt with, she didn't expect him to be involved in the nitty-gritty of planning the exhibition.

Why did the thought displease her?

She blinked, barely catching the last bit of the curator's remark. "I'm sorry, Mrs Sauda, I drifted off for a moment."

"No need for apologies, Princess Edina. I'm sure you have more important things to think about than Mr Asanti's looks."

Edina laughed at the faint blush colouring the other woman's cheeks. Thank God for her own dark complexion, which did a better job of masking her emotions while a wave of exhilaration flowed through her.

They spent some time discussing ideas for the exhibition. As a curator herself, she shared her experiences and strategies she'd used in boosting tourism and getting wider public interest locally and internationally. By the time they parted ways, they'd outlined additional opportunities whereby their two cultural institutes could collaborate.

As she walked through the empty corridors towards her office, she passed doors to several private reading rooms. Some visitors preferred those to the larger libraries in the building. Her mind continued buzzing with ideas. The Bagumi Institute for Research and Cultural Heritage was larger than the Royal Museum of Umaasie, which brought both challenges and opportunities.

As she reached one door that stood ajar, a sound coming from inside made her stop. She frowned, identifying it as someone moaning as if in pain. Alarmed, she pushed the door open and ventured in.

"Hello?"

She stopped abruptly when she found the source of the sound.

Kal?

He lay asleep on a lounge chair, his feet propped up on a matching ottoman. The tome he must have been reading lay on the floor. Her initial shock of setting eyes on him fizzled into alarm when his heavy breathing and tortured sounds reached her. Was he having a bad dream?

"No ... no," he kept mumbled while writhing.

His movements became more agitated as though struggling with someone. She didn't think, or she might have retreated and allowed his nightmare to run its course. She vaguely remembered reading that not getting involved was the best course of action. How could she, though, when she couldn't bear to watch him suffer? Shutting the door, she rushed to his side, hesitating a moment before touching his shoulder and shaking him.

"Kal?"

"What—"

He jerked awake, flinging his arms in a defensive manner. The impact sent her sprawling on her ass with a gasp. He cast a wide gaze around, appearing savage and lost and sexy.

"It's okay," she said. "It's me."

His eyes locked on her and widened, the fierceness receding. As she attempted to rise, he rushed to her aid.

"Forgive me, Princess," he said, helping her up and leading her to the chair he'd just vacated.

She tried to ignore the twinge in her chest at his continued use of the honorific. After their ... uhm ... conversation in the woods the other day, she'd thought they'd forged some level of amity. At least today, though, the word didn't sound like an insult.

He settled on the ottoman, facing her. "Are you all right?"

"I'm fine," she assured him and found herself taking too much pleasure in the relief flooding his face. "You?"

He nodded. "I must have been more exhausted than I realised."

"Exhausted? It's barely lunchtime."

He shut his eyes and sucked in a breath. When he looked at her again, she saw the fatigue. Her fingers itched to touch him again, but she resisted the urge.

"Aren't you sleeping well?"

He gave a snort. "I don't sleep."

She laughed, expecting to hear him follow suit. He didn't, and her expression fizzled into concern. "You're serious."

Several beats passed before he spoke, and even then, he didn't look at her.

"What you just saw? It's worse at night."

He looked at her then, his expression tortured, and the implication of his words sank in.

"Are you saying you don't sleep at all?"

Even as the words came out, she refused to believe them. How could anyone function without sleep?

"Not if I can help it, but it catches up with me." Ridiculously, he attempted a smile. "I pay the price and move on."

His matter-of-fact tone caused more alarm than relief. This had obviously gone on long enough for him to see it as normal. Unacceptable.

"What do you do at night?"

"I work," he said as though it were the most natural thing in the world.

"What about sleeping pills? Surely, those will help you get a good night's rest."

He angled his torso to face her more fully. "Have you ever been held under water against your will?"

She blinked. Instinct told her this wasn't a random question. The thought of someone being cruel to him pumped anger into her and punctured her resistance. She took his hand.

He stared at their linked fingers. She expected him to pull away, but he didn't.

"Artificial aids just impede my ability to wake up. It's like drowning."

Her heart ached for him. Who would have done such a wicked thing to him? He exhaled a heavy breath, extricating his hands from her grip and burying his face in his palms. Then, he rubbed his temples as if warding off a headache.

"How long has this been going on?"

Several seconds ticked by as silence met her inquiry. A wiser woman would have left well enough alone and hightailed it out of there. She'd rescued him from his nightmare. Time to move on.

"Talk to me, Kal."

Apparently, her brain hadn't received the memo to vamoose.

"Let it go, Princess."

Their gazes clashed. She didn't back down. He blinked, clearing the darkness lurking in the silvery grey of his eyes. His jaw clenched. Everything about his demeanour projected reluctance. She expected him to deflect, but she wouldn't have it. Given the path drawn for her, this moment wouldn't repeat itself. Instinct told her he could use a listening ear. Perhaps she, too, needed this in order to move on.

"How long?" she gritted out.

Seconds ticked by, and then, he sighed. "Nearly a year."

His voice was low. She'd have missed it if she hadn't been paying attention. Alarm shot through her. In sharp contrast to her shock, he shrugged.

"What happened nearly a year ago?" she asked.

His eyes blazed with pain and anger the intensity of which stole her breath. She sensed neither emotion was directed at her, however.

"My mother took her own life."

She gasped. The rawness of his voice plunged her into helplessness. A deep yearning to hold him close assailed her, though she knew it wouldn't abate his pain. She could only hope to soothe him in some way.

He cleared his throat. "I've never confessed it out loud."

"Oh, Kal. I don't know what to say."

"Your being here is enough."

She stared at him, amazed at his tenacity even in his brokenness. Meanwhile, moisture flooded her eyes. She blinked. *A princess must never display emotions of weakness in public.* Regardless of the rule, hot streams flowed down her cheeks. She turned away.

"Here," he said. "Take this."

She received the handkerchief he offered and dabbed her eyes and cheeks. As she returned it, she noted the stain from her foundation and eyeliner.

"I must look a mess," she said, imagining how much she'd smudged her make-up despite her best efforts.

"A minuscule smear. Neither that nor tears can mar your beauty."

His eyes held her in a trance as thoughts and desires she couldn't voice swirled within her.

"I wasn't entirely honest with you," he confessed. "There were two weeks during which I had uninterrupted sleep."

"That's wonderful." It surprised her how elated his admission made her. "You just need to recall what you did differently and replicate it."

"That's the thing, Honey Eyes. The difference was you."

Utter silence ensued. Memories surged in. Flutters invaded her belly, reminding her of every kiss they'd shared, every touch, every minute ...

Snapping back to awareness, she admonished herself. The wise thing would be to leave now, but curiosity and opportunity made a heady combination. She'd never get the chance to learn more about him. Not like this. She just had to keep from veering into dangerous territory.

"Tell me about her," she found herself prying. "Your mother. If you don't mind."

The tension around his shoulders eased while the intensity of his expression shifted. His eyes and brows settled in a contemplative expression.

"Mamaa was complex. She functioned on rigid routines. As I grew up, I realised the schedules helped with her mood swings. She was prone to them." He frowned. "She was still the strongest, and wisest, person I've ever known."

A beat passed, and she feared that was all he'd volunteer. She waited, hoping her silence would prompt him to go on. Her instinct turned out to be right.

"Right down to her last breath, everything she ever did was for me," he continued. "No matter what silly question I asked as a kid or what difficulty I faced as an adult, she always had an answer. She had a repertoire of proverbs and wise sayings."

A chuckle left his lips. It occurred to her she hadn't heard a genuine laugh from him since meeting again. The effect of that sound on her system proved devastating. She swallowed.

He was smiling again, staring ahead of him. "'Don't look where you fell, Kal, but where you slipped' or 'Be wise, Rahim. No one tests the depth of a river with both feet.'"

She quirked a brow. "Rahim?"

He jerked his head in her direction, appearing mildly confused by her remark. "My middle name is Ibrahim."

"Aren't they two separate names?"

He nodded. "She still favoured Rahim as an abbreviated form. Our little secret."

She chuckled. "Her wise words make her sound a little like my mother. 'A princess always puts her best foot forward,' 'duty above all else.' She encouraged me to pursue higher education because, 'a queen must be wise and strive for knowledge.'"

Their gazes reconnected, and they both laughed.

"You see, we have more in common than you thought."

Time faded as he told her about the woman whose loss had obviously created a hole in his life. Nearly a year had passed, and yet, his pain still appeared so raw. They traded stories and laughter. Each time he spoke, she listened, absorbing the cadence of his deep voice, her heart aching ... soaring ... falling. For him.

"You're different," he said after a moment. "You're inherently good. You hold no guile or vanity."

"What makes you so sure?"

"I've looked into you," he confessed, eyes blazing with both apology and defiance. "It's a natural hazard of my work and the life I've had."

Seconds ticked by while she grappled with whether to be offended or curious. "Whatever you want to know about me, you can just ask."

"I know that now, but when we met again, we both had reason to mistrust the other."

Heat suffused her face at the memory of her accusations. She couldn't fault him for researching her. After all, hadn't she done the same? Except, she had a feeling he'd been more thorough.

"Why did you mistrust me?"

"Anyone associated with the Saenes is of interest to me."

"The Saenes are good people." She wasn't sure why she'd felt it necessary to say it, but the thought had been insistent in her mind. She'd learnt a long time ago to heed the little voice in her head. Yet, Kal's unconvinced look put doubt in her mind. "Aren't they?"

"They've been an influential family for generations. People with that much power tend to have big secrets. Sometimes, those come with disastrous consequences, and it's always the little guy who suffers."

"Is that why you're here? To save the little guy?"

"If need be."

He spoke with such gravity, she frowned.

"Are you truly saying the Saenes have some terrible secret?"

"If they do, I'll find out soon enough."

She started to say something, but he rose to his feet. She sensed him closing off.

"I should return to my reading now." By the time he'd completed the sentence, he stood at the door. "Thank you for listening. I haven't allowed myself to remember my mother like this."

Rising, she covered the distance between them. Another insistent urge propelled her to stop in front of him.

"Give me your hand."

His brows snapped together, but he did as she requested.

She pulled out a pen from her pocket and scribbled her private number in his palm. "If you ever need to talk about her again, call me."

He stared at the number for a long moment before turning intense eyes on her. "On one condition."

Her brows drew together, a warning ringing in her head. Whatever he meant to ask, it would be something significant, something she might not be able to give. She should say no right now. But ... if there was a chance she could help, shouldn't she at least try?

"Name it."

"I requested a visit to the excavation sites. If it's approved, come with me."

Her breath flowed out in a flood of relief, making her almost laugh at her initial panic. Such a trip would require at least one guide at the site and some staff from the BIRCH, which made his request nowhere near as scandalous as she'd imagined. God, she needed to lighten up around him.

"The photos are great, but seeing it in person will provide better inspiration for the exhibition design I have in mind."

"Is that a yes, then?"

"Yes." Her concerns now alleviated, she allowed herself some excitement. "When?"

"As soon as I get permission. It will be an overnight trip."

"Perfect."

It really was. They'd be back with a few days spare before her two weeks were over. After that, she'd return to her real life where courtship and planning towards her nuptials would eat up most of her free time.

"Perfect is correct," he said.

One corner of his lips lifted in the sexy smile that always put butterflies in her tummy. She steeled herself against the deliciously improper sensations skittering down her spine and forming a heated pool in her nether regions.

"I, uhm … I have to go."

***

Kal sat in his guest suite unable to concentrate on the work he'd set out to do. The rush he normally experienced when assessing a potential acquisition was starkly missing.

His mother's fashion design label, Yadira Designs, had been in a legal battle with a company that constantly stole their creations. Since getting the owner to do the right thing had yielded dismal results, they'd decided to acquire the company outright. It would be the perfect strategy to launch a diffusion line for their label, something Mamaa had talked about but never got around to doing.

Given the connection to his mother, this exercise should have been damn-near euphoric. Instead, his mind kept drifting to the woman whose mere presence filled him with calm and hope and a desire to relinquish control, to let things happen. He hardly made friends, didn't divulge intimate details about his life to anyone. One look from Edina, and he'd found himself spilling his guts.

He'd been tense ever since stepping foot in Bagumi. Being physically close to King Ibrahim had charged his emotions more than expected. Meeting Edina again should have calmed him. Instead, the discovery of her identity had served to fray the edges of his composure.

Yesterday had been different. They'd connected as they had the first time, as if nothing else mattered and no one stood between them. It solidified his conviction that their meeting wasn't a random act of nature. They were meant to be more.

The handkerchief she'd used burnt a hole in his pocket. He'd had to fight the temptation to tie it around his nose. Though she'd possessed it only a few seconds, her scent had imprinted on it.

He didn't know how many times he'd gone over their conversation this morning. She'd seen him in a vulnerable state. Instead of pity or rejection, she'd offered sympathy and help. He'd never known anyone like her. His whole life, he'd been exposed to people who'd take advantage of a vulnerable person.

Like his step-father. They'd met him a couple of years after clawing their way out of abject poverty. Owing to the kindness of an old woman they'd helped during one of the early-June rainstorms Accra was known for, Mamaa gained admission into an apprenticeship with a renowned fashion designer.

Hard work and determination had paid off when she'd graduated and her boss had invited her to showcase some of her own designs in a fashion show. His step-father had been attending the show to find new pieces for his shop. He'd been impressed with her work and commissioned some designs. He'd soon grown enamoured with her. What had started out as a professional relationship soon became more. At eight years of age, Kal hadn't been happy. Another man in their lives meant his real father wouldn't come.

For Mamaa, it had been a strategic alliance. He'd always suspected she'd married the man for his money—part of her plan to give Kal a better life.

A year after they'd married, they hadn't conceived. His step-father had consulted a soothsayer who'd apparently told him the spiritual bond between Mamaa and Kal's biological father was too strong. As long as Kal—the manifestation of this bond—lived, Mamaa would never bear his step-father a child. That was when he'd attempted to drown Kal while bathing him.

He'd never been a good parent, anyway. He'd wanted the woman but never had time for her child. His attempt to get rid of Kal had been the last straw. They'd left him. Years later, Kal had taken utmost pleasure in buying the man's company. The experience had probably been the reason Mamaa never married Shaka's father.

A shrill sound brought him out of those thoughts. It took him a moment to realise it was an alarm he'd set to pick up Shaka from the airport. He grabbed his phone and tapped the 'Dismiss' signal.

Talking to Edina had left him raw, opened the door to memories he'd locked away to then toss the keys. He needed to reel them all back in and focus on the next few days. He'd been invited to the royal family's weekly dinner where the king intended to reveal the news about Kal. There'd be a medical team to take buccal samples for the paternity test.

He needed his brother, not only for moral support but to ensure the samples didn't get tampered with. King Ibrahim might seem happy about the news, but it could all be an act. The man, as well as the family, had every motive to influence the outcome of the test to make him out to be a liar.

As he prepared to set off for the airport, he wondered how Edina would take the news. Should he have forewarned her? He'd been tempted after sharing details of his childhood. One thought had stopped him. This was too delicate a piece of information to put into the wrong hands.

It didn't matter how much he liked her. If she had to choose between him and the Saenes, he didn't know who she'd side with. As long as she still felt any allegiance to them, she couldn't fully be in his confidence. He couldn't afford to mess this up. Not even for her.

Chapter Fourteen

Edina had been invited to the Saenes' weekly family dinner, the first after restrictions on gatherings had been eased several weeks ago. If dinners in her home were anything to go by, then the dress code would be semi-formal to formal. She chose a simple asymmetrical dress that ended a few inches above her knees at the front and mid-calf at the back.

Lace and diamante detail on the bodice elevated the high-neck design from chic to elegant. Her shoes, purse, and nose mask matched the outfit's burgundy colour. She'd gone for smoky eyes with minimal foundation owing to the mask. Satisfied with her look, she headed out.

Arriving at the large dining room, her eyes widened as she took in the attendees. All the king's children were present, including Princess Isha—now the first lady of the Republic of Wanai, and Princess India—now, Queen India of Sudar. They must have flown in earlier today.

Princess Amira, the king's youngest child, came up to her at the door. They'd met on her first day in Bagumi and had seemed to hit it off.

"Love the dress," Amira said.

At four months pregnant and just beginning to show, the Bagumian princess glowed.

"Thanks. I like yours, too," Edina replied.

"Come on. I'll introduce you to my sisters."

They were her half-siblings—Queen Sapphire's children together with Zik—while Amira belonged to Queen Zulekha. The introductions were brief but warm, and once done, they drifted into a conversation on various topics concerning the countries represented by the four of them.

A prickling at the back of her neck caused her to turn, and her gaze clashed with Kal's as he entered. She blinked. He was a guest, too, so she shouldn't be surprised to see him. Still, a nervous shiver ran up her spine. Even though he'd assured her no video of them existed, doubt snuck into her heart. Some of their encounters this past week had been less than innocent. What if he'd misled her into a false sense of security before landing his *coup de grâce*?

The announcement of king and queens heralded the end of pre-dinner chit-chat and her agitated thoughts.

As all the meals she'd had during her stay in Bagumi, dinner was sumptuous—a three-course affair punctuated by congenial conversation. Avoiding stuffing herself proved an uphill task with the selection of local and international dishes bursting with aromas and flavours. Preventing her gaze from drifting over to Kal proved even more difficult.

When dinner ended and the staff had cleared the dessert plates, the king stood. All conversations ceased.

"As some of you are aware, I have an important announcement," he said.

All eyes were riveted on him. Expressions varied from concern to curiosity to expectation.

"Most of you have met Mr Kalahari Asanti. For the benefit of those who haven't, he's the CEO of Asanti Industries. His organisation has reached an agreement with the crown to provide funding to the Bagumi Institute of Research and Cultural Heritage."

Inevitably, her gaze trailed to him. The king had paused. She didn't know why her nerves went on high alert.

"Also, Kalahari is my son."

What?

Her heart bottomed out as gasps echoed across the table. Everyone's focus had shifted to Kal and then back to King Ibrahim. Her attention didn't deviate from Kal who had turned to meet her gaze, his face an unreadable mask.

The king's son? As if a veil had been lifted off her eyes, she saw the resemblance. Kal could have been a younger version of King Ibrahim. Complete silence filled the room for several seconds before Amira burst out.

"He's our brother?"

"Is there proof of this?" Isha asked.

"I have a medical team on stand-by to take swabs."

"Who's his mother?" India asked, her voice controlled, but it didn't fully conceal her incredulity.

She and her siblings were all probably working out the fact that their father had gone outside his marriage vows. Though with two wives, the man wasn't exactly a one-woman man.

"Her name was Yara. She used to live here."

"Was?" one of the sons asked.

A vise formed around her throat, preventing the easy passage of air. Her hands began trembling, prompting her to clasp them on her lap, hidden from view. As the family continued firing questions at the king, her eyes never left Kal's even though his look gave nothing away.

Then she remembered. As far as anyone here knew, she'd only met him a few days ago. This news shouldn't mean a thing to her. Yet, she couldn't breathe, couldn't stop her world from screeching to a halt. Her eyes prickled, her lips quivering in tow. She needed to get out of there.

Before she could, however, Kal rose, and silence expanded over the table as all eyes turned to him, shattering the illusion she'd conjured. He and she had no special connection. His presence had the same halting effect on everyone else.

"I know what a shock this news must be to you," he said. "I felt the same way when I learnt the truth."

Even now, her heart danced and her body thrilled to the melody of his voice. He didn't spare her a glance as his gaze went round the table, pausing on everyone present. Except her.

"I'm here to do a job, and more importantly, to bury my mother. Whatever you feel about who I am, I hope you'll grant me the grace and privacy to say a final goodbye to her."

"As I told you, Kalahari, my son, it's granted," King Ibrahim said.

She couldn't take it anymore. She rose, mumbling something which in her head was an excuse to use the ladies' room.

"Are you all right?" Zik, seated next to her, whispered.

She nodded quickly and hastened out, putting as much distance between herself and the dining room.

***

Kal wished he could chase after Edina, but he stayed behind to play the role of prodigal son. He edged her out of his mind, knowing the respite wouldn't last as he took in the looks on the faces surrounding him. The two queens appeared unfazed, which led him to believe their husband had already informed them. Good for him. The sons—Zawadi, Zik, Zediah, and Zareb—had varying degrees of mistrust on their faces, while Amira and India couldn't seem to hide their hurt and apparent confusion. The oldest sister, Isha, like the queens, appeared unsurprised.

None left an unexpected mark on his soul as had the look on Edina's face when the king had made the announcement. Something in him wanted to have told her earlier, prepared her for the roller-coaster of events to come. He reminded himself why he was here, who she was ... remembered the disgust on her face. Perhaps that had been his real reason for not telling her. He hadn't wanted to witness her reaction to his new status—an illegitimate.

He returned his attention to the conversation around him.

"Our support and love for each other is one of the things that makes this family strong," King Ibrahim was saying. "I'm asking all of you to extend him the same love and consideration you have for each other."

The king diverted his gaze to the others, pausing on each one in turn. "I've fully accepted him, and I hope you will, too. Once the DNA results confirm it, he'll be bestowed with the legitimacy of being my son."

Kal went completely still as the last eight words vibrated through him. Everything seemed to be falling into place. By all appearances, Ibrahim was truly happy to have been united with him. Regardless, discomfort settled firmly in his gut. He knew exactly why.

Too easy. Maybe things fell into place without a hitch for people like the Saenes, but Mamaa had had to fight for everything she got. Consequently, he'd grown up cultivating a healthy dose of scepticism whenever anything came with little difficulty, a trait which made him a formidable success in his career. He could easily look beyond the politics and BS of organisations and nations alike to make sound analyses and take action.

"What?"

Zawadi's shocked response brought Kal back to the present.

The former crown prince rose, hostility rolling from him as he aimed narrowed eyes at his father and then at Kal. "Legitimacy? What does that actually mean?"

Kal's attention inadvertently sought out the others, taking in Zik's discrete snort of disbelief. Zareb, who seemed to keep his emotions close to his chest, revealed nothing facially, while his twin, Zediah, seemed to appraise Kal with new eyes.

"This only means you have a new brother," the king said in an almost pained voice. "Kalahari is as much my son as any of you."

"So, naturally, we're simply to welcome him with open arms?" Isha asked. "The king has spoken."

"You've accepted and love each other even though you don't all come from the same mother. What's different about Kalahari?"

Zik shook his head. "It isn't that simple, Baba."

"Besides, the rest of us grew up together," Zediah said. "As far as we're concerned, Kalahari is a stranger."

It occurred to him that Zareb hadn't voiced an opinion since the announcement had been made. On the surface, he didn't appear as vexed as the others, but Kal knew better than to make assumptions about his silence. The head of palace security bore the calculated look of someone already formulating a counteraction. Kal expected nothing less.

While listening to the exchange, he studied and made observations about his half-siblings and their mothers. He might need insider support for the next step of his plan. This meeting presented an excellent opportunity to suss out possible allies and enemies.

"When paternity is confirmed—"

"Don't you mean if, Baba?" Zareb cut in.

Silent seconds ticked by. His father straightened his posture, squared his shoulders, king replacing father.

"I've asked Tianah to set up a short press conference to present Kalahari to the nation after the reading of the results. Amira and India, make sure your brother has something suitable to wear."

They both nodded, then Amira rose. "May we be excused?"

With the king's permission, the two left the room, Amira's husband in tow.

Isha rose and walked straight to Kal. "Welcome to the family, Kalahari. Although, you may discover you might have been better off keeping your old one."

Kal gave her an acknowledging nod. This was one of those situations where wisdom lay in silence.

Zareb stood next and aimed a hard look his way. "If you aren't who you say you are, I'll make you suffer."

He didn't back down from the other man's hostility. "You'll soon find out I'm not given to speaking lies."

Zareb grunted before offering his hand to his fiancée, Malika, seated next to him. As they left, the rest of the family filed out with a couple of them pausing to give Kal a pseudo-welcome. Moments later, he remained alone with the king.

"That went well," the older man commented.

Kal frowned at the king's dismal attempt at humour. He should stick to ruling. On second thought, he decided Ibrahim might not be joking. For news which could potentially upend their lives, Kal had anticipated more hostility from the family. Just as with Ibrahim's reaction, things seemed to have gone too smoothly at dinner. Except for Edina. She couldn't stomach the idea of being in the same room. Why else would she hurry out of there, away from him, the moment the news had been announced?

He clenched his jaw, swallowing back the bile rising up his throat, then returned his gaze to the king. Was Ibrahim being genuine, or did he plan to play a role to an anticipated devastating end?

CHAPTER FIFTEEN

Back in her chambers forty minutes later, Edina fought to quell her trembling hands. Her mind and body still buzzed, unable to contain the shock to her system.

Kalahari … a prince! In trying to have one wild night, she'd gravitated towards exactly what she'd been running from. The irony of it.

Why hadn't he told her? He'd had more than one opportunity to do so, but he hadn't taken it. She meant nothing to him, so she had no right to feel betrayed or hurt, and yet, she did. That day in the woods, she'd opened up to him, while he'd chosen to keep this monumental thing from her.

Her phone rang, the sound piercing through her muddled thoughts. She grimaced upon seeing her brother's name flashing across the screen. She was ten minutes late for the scheduled check-in. She let it go to voicemail, knowing Barimah would cut and dial again without leaving a message.

By the time the device chirped again, she'd composed herself enough for it. She tapped the icon for a video call. It was the next best thing after face-to-face, her brother's preference.

"Good evening, Barimah."

"Good evening, *Owoahene*." Her brother frowned. "Are you okay?"

Her heart swelled with affection at her brother's concern. She'd never been in doubt about his love for her. Right now, she soaked it up and didn't even care that he'd joined the '*Owoahene*' bandwagon.

"I'm fine," she assured him. "I just had some surprising news."

"I trust nothing bad."

She had no idea how to classify the news of Kal's true identity, but there was only one correct response to Barimah's question. "No. Just surprising."

"Are you on course with your assignments in Bagumi?"

She nodded. "I've had two meetings with King Ibrahim and Prince Azikiwe. The outcome was positive."

"Good, good." He leant back in his seat. "I had a lengthy conversation with your intended this morning. He's eager to meet you upon your return."

She groaned.

"What was that?"

"Nothing," she said quickly. "How's my beautiful sister-in-law and the children?"

"They're fine." He broke into a smile, no doubt brought on by the mention of his family, but his next words made it clear he didn't intend to drop the conversation. "I see you haven't warmed to the idea of your engagement. Perhaps when you meet, you'll have a change of heart. I found him to be pleasant enough."

Pleasant enough. What every woman dreamt of.

"Edina, you cannot be 'Mother of Kings' without a husband."

"I don't need to marry to have children."

"Be serious," he said in a firm big-brother voice. His look softened when her attempt at keeping a straight face failed and a smile escaped. "Marriage isn't a death sentence, you know."

She scoffed. "Easy for you to say. You and Mahalia are perfect for each other."

He cocked his brows. "We didn't come out of the box like this, you know."

"What are you talking about? Didn't you say you fell for her the moment you saw her?"

"I did." He gave her a contemplative look. "You know how they say success is ten percent talent and ninety-percent hard work?"

She nodded.

"Well, the same applies to marriage. Ten percent love, ninety percent commitment. Merging two interests, upbringings, ambitions, cultures ... you name it ... takes hard work."

"More so for some than others."

Barimah stared at her for a long moment. "I'm going to tell you something. You won't repeat this to anyone."

"Not everything has to be an edict, Your Majesty. I see you're home. Within those walls, your role as brother, husband, and father supersedes that of king."

"Promise, or this conversation ends now."

"Fine. You have my word."

He exhaled. "Our wedding night was a disaster."

"Whoa, I don't want to hear about your sex life."

"I wouldn't volunteer this information if I didn't think my humiliation would give you perspective."

He seemed so serious, she had no option than to listen. "Okay."

"It wasn't just our first night. For months, I couldn't please her, and it wasn't for lack of skill. I made the mistake of assuming my previous experiences had prepared me for my wife. I discovered how wrong I was when I found her one evening pleasuring herself."

Her eyes widened. The last thing she wanted occupying space in her mind was her brother's marital intimacies, but curiosity held her by the reins.

"What did you do?"

"I was furious at first. I knew I was yet to give her an orgasm, but I hadn't realised how deprived she was. I wanted her to be happy, and knowing I was failing her in this very important aspect of our lives humbled me. Eventually, I had to put aside my pride and ask her to show me what to do."

"Show you?"

"Exactly what you're thinking."

He smiled. It was one she hadn't seen on his face before. For the first time, she saw him not as her big brother or any of his multiple designations. She saw him as a man.

An image of pleasuring herself while Kal watched flashed through her mind. Her skin flushed, and her throat suddenly went dry. Oh, God. How could she be thinking about him? She coughed, turning away.

"I didn't mean to shock you."

"I'm okay, but enough with the sex talk."

She had to admit, speaking with her brother had brought some calmness to her. She no longer felt like the Earth had disappeared from under her feet.

"All I wanted to get across was even when you meet someone you love or are attracted to, happiness doesn't just happen."

She didn't want to talk about this or argue with her brother, so she opted for a conciliatory approach. "So you're saying I should just marry your Ghanaian chief and work hard at being happy with him."

Her trick worked.

Barimah's stiff shoulders dropped as he sighed. "Just keep an open mind. Don't leave the fate of the kingdom to Zora."

She saw concern on his face, which softened her. Focusing so hard on her own happiness had been selfish. It had made her lose sight of the big picture.

She nodded. "Okay."

When the call ended, she continued to mull over it. Perhaps Barimah had a point. If love made everything else fall into place, wouldn't Kal have confided in her? She nearly laughed. Expecting his trust assumed he reciprocated her feeling. Clearly, he didn't. Right now, she couldn't help wondering what else he had up his sleeve.

***

A bright, sunny morning poured in through egress windows, a sharp contrast to Kal's mood. Heeding Shaka's advice, he hadn't spent the night at the palace. The combination of Mamaa being gone and the DNA results pending placed him in a no-man's-land. Safety-wise, he was at his most vulnerable. Everyone who could possibly feel threatened by his identity resided at the palace, with easy access to him if he'd stayed.

Unwilling to be a sitting duck for his potential enemies, he'd agreed to lay low for the next four days until he had to return for the reading of the DNA results.

Shaka had brought a few of Kal's clothes in anticipation of a scenario like this, so he hadn't even passed by his room to pack a bag. He'd left the dinner table and headed to a waiting vehicle, which had brought him to the safe house.

Given the ceiling-level windows, they were in the basement. From what he'd seen last night when they'd arrived, the main building was unassuming, occupied by a middle-aged couple who provided a good cover.

So here he was. He'd been staring at the overhead fan for nearly an hour, unable to motivate himself to get out of the bed which had lived up to his expectation of being uncomfortable.

He abhorred the waiting, loathed that the next step of his plan rode on something he had absolutely no control over. Discomfort locked in his chest. The same feeling had occurred last night when the swab had touched the inside of his cheek. He'd recognised it immediately. Doubt.

He'd taken his mother's word for it. She'd never given him reason to question her—not on something this important. King Ibrahim's apparent eagerness exacerbated the feeling, making him wonder about the king's motives.

What did the man hope the outcome would be? Were his expectations strong enough for him to doctor the result to his fit his objective? Were their wishes aligned in this one instance? The questions hadn't stopped plaguing his mind and only got worse since he had nothing but time on his hands.

A knock sounded at the door, rousing him out of his thoughts.

"Come in."

The door opened, and Shaka entered, the smell of freshly brewed coffee hot on his heels.

Kal raised his brows as he took in the steaming mug in his brother's hand. "You brought me coffee?"

"You wish." As if to buttress his point, Shaka settled against the door jamb and took a long sip. "You want coffee, haul your ass out there, and pour yourself a cup. Now if you're done pining over the princess, maybe we can talk."

He rolled to a seating position and tried to ignore the stirring in his groin at the mention of Edina. He'd made a conscious effort to refrain from thinking about her. He'd failed miserably. Try as he might, he couldn't forget the expression in her eyes when the king had made the announcement—a look akin to disgust—so different from those she'd given him the night they'd met or even the day in the museum library.

He supposed being with a commoner had been the thrill for her. Apparently, a commoner was more desirable than what he now was in her eyes— illegitimate. She'd hightailed it out of the dining room at the first opportunity, buttressing his conviction.

He curled his fingers in. He did *not* want to think about her. It would exacerbate the ache in his chest. Unfortunately, his mind appeared to have no intention of relinquishing thoughts of her. Instead, it played out memories of the desire in her eyes when she'd incited him to kiss her in the garden, the way she'd wrapped her arms around him and returned his kiss ... her moans. What look would she give him when they found themselves in bed together again?

The sound of Shaka snapping his fingers reeled him back. "I guess you aren't done."

He swore silently, realising the inevitable effect of his thoughts on his morning erection.

"I'll be out in ten," he said.

"Take fifteen, and get your head straight. Once you step out of this room, I don't want you spacing out."

He forced a smile, determined not to succumb to his baser instinct of punching his brother in the face. "I'm all in."

With a snort of laughter, Shaka left the room.

And just for that, Kal set a timer and ensured he stepped out with a minute to spare. He found

Shaka in the space serving the multiple purposes of living and dining area with a kitchenette wedged in one corner. Stopping at the counter, he poured himself a cup of coffee and joined Shaka at the table.

For several moments, his brother stared at him, eyes narrowed.

"What?"

"This trip hasn't gone as planned."

"Agreed."

The objective of this first trip had been to gather information and establish contacts close to the crown. He hadn't planned on revealing the truth about his paternity. The decision had been taken out of his hands, however, when the king had approached him. He couldn't have denied it then and later returned to claim it.

"And maybe that's not a bad thing," Shaka said with an inflection as if it were a question. "You look less … stressed. It's because of her, isn't it?"

He couldn't help smiling. Unquestionably, the best surprise of this trip was reconnecting with Edina. He couldn't have predicted that in his wildest dreams. Just like on New Year's Eve, being in her presence—even the fact of being in the same city at the same time during a global pandemic— felt inevitable. Fated. Now that he had, he wouldn't let her slip through his fingers.

He just had to convince her that, illegitimate or not, he was the one for her.

CHAPTER SIXTEEN

Edina knew better than to pat herself on the back for surviving the past three days. She'd done so without setting eyes on Kal. In her defence, she hadn't made a deliberate effort to avoid him. She'd learnt he hadn't stayed at the palace since dinner the other night.

It was a good thing. No Kal to evoke emotions best kept hidden. No heated looks to awaken memories of their night together. No stolen kisses to turn her knees to jelly or riddle her heart with self-reproach.

He'd nonetheless appeared in her dreams, uncompromising in his desire. He'd whispered naughty things in her ears, touching her in ways that made her yearn and squirm in the queen-sized bed. She'd woken up several times in the course of each warm tropical night drenched in sweat, her centre pulsing with need … and a serving of guilt on the side. The cold showers every morning had done nothing to douse the fire of her awakened desire.

No escape from Kal-related emotional upheaval today, though. She'd spent the entire morning concocting possible excuses to abstain from the announcement of the DNA results. Yet, she knew if such a justification presented itself, she'd find reasons to reject it.

Despite her wish to avoid all contact with him, she needed to be there, needed to hear first-hand whether he'd become a permanent fixture in her life. It would be fate's perfect revenge for taking matters into her own hands in defiance of her obligation. Or maybe, for a number of inexplicable reasons, she simply wanted to lay eyes on him again.

Was he okay? Had his sleep pattern worsened from anxiety? He had to be sure about his claim to come forward and avail himself to a paternity test. But what if he was wrong?

She shook off the thoughts and focused on getting ready. Hiding her emotions behind a veil of make-up, she surveyed her wardrobe options. While expending her energies on her ongoing work at the museum as she tried to stem thoughts of Kal, she hadn't spared a thought on what to wear today.

Thankfully, her ladies' maid had laid out four outfits for her to choose from. She settled on a lavender-coloured blouse paired with an elegant white trouser suit that accentuated her curves. In corporate circles, it might have been called a power suit.

A knock sounded at her door. They must have sent someone to escort her to the throne room where the announcement would take place.

"Just a second," she called out.

Slipping on a nose mask and her designer stilettos, she picked up the matching purse and opened the door.

She reared back, unable to conceal her surprise when she found Princesses Amira and India with two personal guards behind them. A third stood beside them. With the exception of the king and queens, the royal family did without bodyguards while on palace grounds.

Her confusion must have shown because India said, "Zareb insists the occasion warrants extra precaution."

"He seems intense," Edina answered.

Amira nodded. "He's gone full OCD."

She smiled, stepping out and securing her door.

The two women wore traditional outfits made from the same fabric, and Edina wondered if she should also have donned something more West African. Too late now.

"Our brothers and Isha are having a pow-wow before the big meeting," Amira informed her. "Zik said you'd walk over on your own, but we thought you'd appreciate the company."

She smiled. "That's very gracious of you."

She noticed a small car parked on the paved road in front of the suite.

"Are we driving?"

Even though the residential sections of the palace were separate from the official areas, she'd planned on walking, which would have taken her ten minutes—perhaps a little more in her six-inch heels.

"Yes. Unless you want to ruin those gorgeous shoes," India replied.

"Good point."

The drive to the administration wing took less than five minutes. They continued with light conversation, which occupied her thoughts for a moment. As soon as the car stopped and they alighted, her heart began thumping.

"What do you think the results are going to be?" she asked.

Amira glanced at her. "To be honest, I don't know. He kind of looks like Baba's photos when he was young, but at the same time, statistically speaking, if we looked hard enough, we could find a few young men who kind of look like our father."

Edina managed a tight smile. She doubted there were any men out there without the surname of Saene who looked like Kal.

"It may not be the worst timing, if you ask me," India continued.

"How so?"

"With Zawadi's abdication and the continued unrest between Bagumi and some of our neighbours, it's best to have all surprises pop up now so they can be dealt with once and for all."

"I suppose you have a point there."

Their conversation ceased as they entered the throne room, a large rectangular setup with ceremonial elegance and splendour. A plush red carpet led from the bubinga double doors to the far end where the throne stood. Unlike in Umaasie where Barimah's throne shared the highest platform with the queen's, King Ibrahim's throne, raised by one step, stood alone while his two queens sat in prominent positions a step lower.

India and Amira led her to sit on the right side with the rest of the royal family. Opposite them sat other members of the royal court. A frightening number of guards stood at the entrances.

She tried not to dwell on the fact that a handful of people wore western attires—none in the royal family, who'd all donned what she'd learnt was the family cloth.

"All rise," the court crier announced, cutting into her musings. "His Majesty, King Ibrahim Saene, is arriving."

They all rose as the monarch entered, majestic in a robe draped over Bagumian traditional clothes and wearing a gold crown adorned with precious stones. In his right hand, he held a sceptre.

Behind him were his royal adviser and three guards who dispersed to their designated positions as the king ascended his throne.

"Bring them in," he instructed.

As the doors swung open, she held her breath, trying to soothe the worry working her insides. Nine people entered, but she had eyes for Kal alone. He was devastating in a tailored charcoal grey work of art—because a suit which looked that good on a man couldn't be described as anything less.

Head held high, shoulders squared, his long, confident strides could have been mistaken for a king about to hold court. He appeared fearless, unperturbed by the half-dozen guards surrounding him. From their formation—two leading, two flanking, and two following—they were clearly not there for his protection.

Her attention moved to the other two people in the group. The first, a short, bespectacled woman looking official in a navy boubou and holding a briefcase. The other, a man wearing a black suit with a white shirt and black tie, looked as burly and intense as any of the uniformed guards.

They directed Kal to stand several feet before the throne. In front of everyone. As if he were on trial.

"Let's begin," the king said.

The royal linguist stepped forward and bowed to the monarch before addressing the gathering.

"Mr Kalahari Asanti, whose mother is Yara Asanti, claims to be the son of King Ibrahim. Our magnanimous ruler has availed himself to a DNA test to ascertain the truth," he started. "If Mr Asanti's claim proves to be false, the law will deal with him appropriately."

The man paused as if to give Kal a chance to change his mind.

Nerves jangled in her belly. She found herself clasping her hands over her lap.

"Dr Dakeh, come forward," King Ibrahim said. "I'm as anxious as any of you to know the results."

Stiff nods and murmurs rippled through the hall in response.

The woman in the navy boubou took out an envelope from her briefcase and raised it as she stepped towards the king.

"Your Majesty, as you can see, these results are still sealed."

"Open it, Dr Dakeh."

Every eye followed the doctor's hands as she ripped open the envelope and took out a sheet of paper.

Edina glanced at Kal. His face remained expressionless, but he had to be a little nervous. What if the results came out negative, proving his claim to be a lie?

Worse—what if he really was Ibrahim's son, but someone had tampered with the results? What would happen to him? She had no doubt he'd be facing some serious charges.

Dr Dakeh's voice brought her back to the present. "With your permission, Your Majesty, I shall read the outcome of the test."

King Ibrahim nodded.

"The results are unequivocal, Your Majesty." The doctor returned her attention to the sheet. "Mr Kalahari Ibrahim Asanti is your son."

Edina's heart did that thing again—the one where it started beating erratically, and she realised she'd stopped breathing. A sudden light-headedness forced her to inhale deeply. She looked around, noting various reactions of surprise expand over the room. Kal's shoulders relaxed, the gesture so slight, it surprised her she'd even noticed.

King Ibrahim smiled and stood.

"Come here, my son." He embraced Kal and placed a signet ring on his little finger.

Her pulse hadn't calmed down despite the number of deep breaths she'd taken. She barely managed to stop her legs from bouncing with their itch to carry her out of there. This being a formal occasion, however, no one could exit until after the king had left or until he'd dismissed the assembly. Besides, anyone who was at dinner the other night might start suspecting something if she ran out again.

In a daze, she watched the rest of the ceremony continue as though she were on the outside looking in.

When the formal event ended, everyone proceeded to a designated banquet hall for a cocktail.

She stood on the side-lines, trying to determine the best opportunity to escape. No matter how hard she tried, her gaze seemed to drift to Kal's location. Presently, he and the king stood side by side with a few royal advisors having a conversation. They were soon interrupted by Queen Zulekha who pulled her husband aside.

Kal turned, facing where she stood. Even from across the hall, his gaze immediately found her, making it clear he'd been fully aware of her position in the room. Pinpricks of awareness heated her face, and her body began to tingle.

His attention didn't waver as he began walking towards her.

Alarm shot through her, forcing her to do what any sane woman would in this situation. She turned and hastened out.

***

Kal went after Edina. He hadn't had a chance to speak with her since this whole thing started nearly a week ago. He should never have blindsided her with his identity. It had been a mistake on his part. He needed to set the record straight before his actions alienated her.

Someone tried to stop him. He heard words of congratulations and mumbled a response as he increased his pace. He exited the banquet hall in time to see Edina turn a corner. Rounding the corner, he caught a glimpse of white disappearing behind a door.

He paused for a second, taking in several deep breaths and willing his heart to calm down before following her in. It was a small tea room, decorated in elegant opulence as the rest of the palace.

She stood a few steps in, her face buried in her hands. She looked stunning in an all-white suit that hugged her in a way that made blood rush to his groin. Most people at the gathering had donned traditional African outfits. She, like him, had chosen the armour of a tailored suit.

She turned the moment the door shut. Surprise registered briefly on her beautiful face before she schooled her expression.

"What are you doing here?" she asked, her voice pure steel. "I suppose you must be addressed as Your Highness. You are, after all, the son of a king."

He hated the animosity in her voice.

"Kal will do just fine."

"You must have had a thousand laughs at my expense, hearing me going on about marrying a man of noble birth, telling me you didn't desire to be a prince when all along, you were planning your big reveal."

"I can explain."

"What's there to explain, Your Highness?"

"Kal."

"What I want to know, *Your Highness,* is why you're doing this when you've been clear about how much you hate royalty and everything that goes with it."

"I can't change my parentage."

"Lucky for you, you never had to reveal your identity. So if you want to explain anything, tell me why you're doing this. You might have everyone fooled with your prodigal son routine, but I'm not buying it. I may have been wrong about you being here because of me, but I know you're up to something."

She glowered at him, but he could see pain in her eyes. The fact that she suspected him of having ulterior motives should have worried him. At the minimum, he should have paused to consider his next move. Right now, however, all he could think about was the petulant curl of her lips and how he wanted to kiss them into submission.

As though she knew exactly where his mind had gone, she turned around, depriving him of her luscious mouth.

"I offered to explain, and you shot me down." Infuriatingly, she continued to face away from him. "Look at me, Princess."

She whipped around. "Say my name!"

The fire in her voice, the moisture in her eyes, caught him by surprise and stole his momentum. The hurt, which he'd placed there, cut him, led him to make himself a promise. He'd never again be responsible for her tears.

"We've been equally dishonest with each other," she continued. "So the least you can do is address me by name."

"Edina."

It rolled out of his mouth like second nature. After all, she was never far from his thoughts.

Her eyes widened as if she hadn't expected him to acquiesce. The atmosphere in the room became charged, and an invisible force propelled him towards her. The next moment, he had her in his arms, her body pressed against him.

"Edina."

He said it softly, savouring every syllable, letting her know how beautiful he found her name.

Her eyes bore into his, and his heart expanded as though she'd reached in and cracked it open. Her soothing effect surrounded him.

"Edina," he whispered.

Now that he'd started, he couldn't seem to stop.

Her tongue slipped out to lick her lips. His throat went dry.

"Don't do that again if you don't want me to kiss you."

Her lips parted with an exhalation. "What if—"

She stopped abruptly.

"Say it, Goddess." He closed the space between them. "I'll give you whatever you want."

"Kal, you don't know what you're asking."

"I'm asking you to be mine." He cupped her face, stroking her cheek with his thumb. "Do you think I like putting myself on display like I just did?"

"Why did you, then?" she whispered.

Like she didn't know.

"Because you need a man with a title."

Surprise sparked in her eyes.

"Kal."

She bit on her lower lip. It wasn't a lick, but it counted in his book. Especially after what she'd stopped herself from saying.

He dipped his head until their lips were inches apart—enough room for her to back out. When she didn't, he closed the space between them.

He'd barely sipped from her lips when the sound of a throat clearing penetrated his consciousness. He stiffened.

With a gasp, Edina tore out of his arms. Horror took over her features as she turned towards the entrance. He did the same as the door clicked shut. Tension eased off him when his gaze met the intruder's.

"Shaka." He turned to Edina. "It's okay. He's my brother."

Shaka maintained an even expression as if he'd walked in on a game of chess. He bowed towards Edina.

"Your Royal Highness." His gaze returned to Kal. "We need to talk."

"I have to go," Edina said.

As she walked past him, Kal caught her arm. "May I call you tonight?"

She paused, and for a second, he thought she'd tell him to never touch her again. Instead, she nodded, and then she was gone.

CHAPTER SEVENTEEN

Kal hadn't realised how full his day would be. After completing the required formalities, he'd been invited to participate in some royal functions and a late lunch with members of the National Council. They were occasions he couldn't afford to miss as these meetings provided a good platform for information he'd ordinarily not be privy to. He was back on track and faring even better than anticipated. He'd soon be in a position to strike King Ibrahim where it hurt the most and he had Edina. All would be right at last.

By the time he returned to the palace, it was nearly six o'clock. He was eager to speak with Edina, but he'd give her a couple of hours to eat and settle down. He calmed the quickening of his heart. A smile touched his lips as he thought about a quiet evening with his woman.

His woman. He liked the sound of that.

Shaking his head, he began to undress. When had he turned into a sappy romantic?

Walking over to the wardrobe, he took out a hanger to place the clothes on. His gaze fell on a box he'd pushed to the back end of the shelf, and he paused. In it sat the urn containing Mamaa's remains. She'd have turned fifty-five tomorrow. Instead, he'd be burying her.

A sudden heaviness descended on him, and his eyes prickled. He gripped the doors of the wardrobe and shut his eyes. He hadn't cried when she'd died. He wasn't about to give in to tears now.

"Why did you do it?" he said in a broken whisper. "He wasn't worthy of you. You had a man who loved you with his whole heart."

Xavier Dubane had loved Mamaa so much, he'd settled for the crumbs left over from the love she'd wasted on Ibrahim. The vicious cycle of unrequited love.

The image of Edina's face flashed through his mind, and warmth filled him.

You'd have liked her, Mamaa.

He hung the clothes and shut the door. The sound echoed with such finality, it nearly crippled him. Going on a year since her passing, he'd finally reached a point where the pain of his loss no longer felt like a dagger lodged in his heart.

Putting distance between himself and the closet didn't improve his mood. He entertained the idea of calling Shaka for a few seconds. If there was one person in the world who could get him out of a funk, it was his brother. But Shaka wasn't the one he wanted to talk to.

His mind drifted right back to Edina. Conversation was the farthest thing from his mind as he remembered the lushness of the lips he'd barely tasted before they'd been interrupted. He checked his time again. It was going to be a long couple of hours.

***

Edina hadn't been this excited since … Had she ever been this eager about anything? The balmy evening air didn't help, acting in league with her nerves to create a light sheen of sweat in her palms despite the air conditioning. If she lowered the temperature any more, she'd be shivering in no time. She squeezed a handkerchief in one hand and then the other. For the umpteenth time, she fought the urge to check her phone. Again.

Kal's message earlier said he'd call at half past nine. She'd been ready thirty minutes early, trying to deceive her impatience with a book she'd been meaning to read for ages. Despite being from one of her favourite authors, it hadn't succeeded in distracting her.

When the call from a private number came through, she answered it immediately.

"Hi."

"Hi." He had a smile in his voice that made her pulse race. "Were you holding the device? It hardly rang."

Her face heated though he couldn't see her.

"Not exactly, but I was waiting."

"Hm, I would've pegged you as a patient woman."

"You're the one person who has this effect on me."

"Good to know." His voice was as soft as a caress. "How was your day?"

"You already know. You saw me today." A flash of excitement spread through her at the memory of what had happened earlier.

"I'm privy to a portion of your day. You'll have to fill me in on the rest."

"Funny," she teased, but went ahead and told him about all the things she'd occupied herself with while counting down to his phone call.

In turn, he told her about the meetings he'd had since they'd parted ways and how he'd wanted her there each step of the way.

She sighed happily. This was so high school, but it felt great, and she didn't waste time overthinking it. They'd started things in reverse order. Despite their soul-deep connection, it was nice to just talk.

"Step outside," he said suddenly.

"Are you ... here?"

She turned towards the door, her ears perking up in expectation of a knock. A thrill shimmied through her belly at the prospect. She chided herself. As a guest of the king and a representative of her country, it wouldn't do for her to be caught in a compromising situation with Kal, especially while the prospect of her engagement remained. But she'd tapped into the entirety of her willpower this morning. If she admitted him into her suite, she'd be begging him to make love with her.

"No," he said, reeling her back from hope to unreasonable disappointment. "Your balcony. I want to show you something."

Curiosity propelled her towards the casement doors leading to her balcony. She slid it open and stepped out, shutting it again. She glanced down, half-expecting to find him standing there. All she saw were the flower gardens, illuminated by solar garden lights. Despite their beauty, she found herself gazing beyond, still searching for him in the dark.

"What did you want me to see?"

"The stars," he said.

"Oh." She tried not to sound disappointed.

"Oh?" he repeated with a questioning inflection, a hint of amusement in his voice. "Excuse me for underwhelming you."

"Sorry. I thought you were here."

"After I said I wasn't?"

She covered her embarrassment with a short laugh. "A girl can hope."

"Honey Eyes, walking away from you this morning was one of the hardest things I've ever done in my life. I need a full day to recuperate."

"I know what you mean."

We'll be together soon.

She made the promise to herself, not wanting to turn this call into a sap-fest.

"What about the stars?"

She gazed up and gasped. This side of the palace transitioned into miles of lush tropical woodlands beyond which lay the Atlantic Ocean. It was beautiful during the day, but at night, it stunned. Undiffused by artificial city lights, the bluish darkness of the night sky spotlighted stars spangled around a gorgeous gibbous moon. Nature's rich tapestry never ceased to amaze.

"When we started out on the streets, there were people who rented out wooden kiosks to the homeless. Sometimes, market women allowed us to pitch a makeshift tent under their stalls, in exchange for cleaning up for them."

Not knowing what to say, she remained quiet, waiting for the rest of the story and how it related to the starry sky.

"Gangs would often raid the various quarters, stealing and forcing themselves on the women." He paused. "My mother was gorgeous."

"Oh, Kal." Her breath hitched with fear of what this story would reveal.

"She was fine," he assured. "The guy hadn't expected Mamaa to be able to defend herself. Apparently, my father had taught her how to fight."

The corners of her lips twitched upwards as relief whooshed out of her. She couldn't help picturing a young King Ibrahim and Kal's mother. She wished she knew what the woman had looked like.

"You called him your father," she remarked.

"What?"

"Never mind. Continue."

After a few seconds, he did.

"I had trouble sleeping after that, so my mother started using food to bribe night watchmen in office buildings in the nearby central business district. They'd let us sleep there until just before dawn."

"She sounds remarkable."

"She was ... complicated," he replied.

This wasn't the first time he'd used those words to describe his mother.

"I digress," he said. "I promise this story has a happy ending."

So many emotions swirled within her, she wished she could reach into the phone and touch him.

"One night—it was my birthday—we couldn't get into any of the three places we normally slept. Someone had reported the night watchmen, and the new guys had been given strict warnings. Mamaa managed to sneak us into a park earmarked for a children's playground. She'd splurged to get some cupcakes and jollof rice with grilled chicken. She sang me happy birthday, and we ate, then slept on our raffia mat under the open sky."

"Was it a starry night like today?"

"Yes. Every time the stars come out like this, I remember that day over twenty years ago. It's still one of my favourite childhood memories."

Her heart both warmed and ached. Kal had been through so much from an early age—things that would break anyone—and yet, he seemed to have derived his strength from those very things. Still, she knew some burdens were better shared.

"I was a teenager when I lost my father," she found herself saying. "I got along much better with him than my mother. He encouraged me to pursue my personal interests while my mother had a path drawn up for me, which was always a sore spot between us because I never listened to her."

"I knew you couldn't have always been the person who follows the rules even to her own detriment."

His remark sounded serious, though softened by its gentle delivery.

"I don't know. It's always been my inclination," she confessed. "My father taught me to explore my individuality, to be me while preparing for my future role as queen. When he died, there was no one to insulate me from my mother's influence. I felt lost."

"How did you cope?" As though he realised he'd asked a loaded question, he added, "If you want to share."

Her first instinct was to take the out he offered, but she was done travelling the safe route. Especially when it came to Kal.

She leaned against the balustrade. "I saw a therapist."

The only person she'd told was Jamila. Though she'd considered Zoraya a friend at the time, she hadn't felt comfortable confiding in her. Perhaps her subconscious had already sensed the shift in her cousin. As future queen, she couldn't afford to be thought of as mentally incapable. At least, her mother had been insistent about it.

"Did it help?"

She breathed out, feeling light for sharing. "I think so. Talking to her helped me work through my feelings and find a balance between what I needed and what was expected. She gave me a safe space to talk and be emotional without judgement until I figured out my path."

Several seconds elapsed.

"Shaka thinks I should see someone," he said quietly. "A sleep therapist, at the very least. He thinks I have too much anger."

"Do you agree?"

"I'm a private person. Keeping things close to my chest is how I've always operated." He sighed audibly. "But he's right about the anger. I've carried it for so long, I don't know how else to feel. It can't have been for nothing."

"Letting go feels anticlimactic," she said.

"Exactly."

"Who are you angry with?"

Seconds ticked off, and she started to wonder if the call had dropped. She checked the screen to confirm they were still connected before placing the device against her ear again.

"You want me to choose you, but you can't be open with me?"

"The king."

"Your father?"

"That man may have sired me, but he holds no fatherly place in my heart. He abused his position and seduced an innocent woman, then exiled her without a penny when she fell pregnant."

She didn't know what to say to that. She wanted to encourage him to hear his father's side of the story, but she had a feeling that advice would roll off his back.

"She would have been fifty-five on Saturday," he said in a low voice. "Instead, I'm burying her."

"Oh, Kal, I'm so sorry."

She'd have given anything to be near him now, holding him tight, though nothing but time would ever truly ease the pain of his loss.

"Will you come?"

"Yes," she said without hesitation.

Seconds ticked off. She remained quiet, sensing he needed a moment.

A yawn drifted over.

"You must be exhausted. You've had a long day. I should let you get some rest."

He didn't protest. "Dinner tomorrow?"

"I can't. Queen Sapphire invited me to dine with her and her children before her daughters return to their homes," she said.

The invitation had come through Zik who, as future king, had assumed the task of playing host to her on behalf of his father.

"Can we talk after?"

She returned to her room, securing the balcony door behind her.

"Do you need to get ready?" he asked. "I can call back."

She shook her head before remembering he couldn't see her. Next time, they'd have to video call.

"No. I just need to change and wrap my hair."

"What do you wear to sleep?"

"A nightie."

"Silk or cotton?"

"Lightweight cotton. I don't like the slippery sensation of silk when I'm sleeping."

"I'm filing that for later analysis."

"Hm. What kind of analysis?"

"You'll find out soon enough." A beat passed. "Will you sleep in the nude tonight? For me?"

Her breath caught.

"Did anyone ever tell you your diction is sometimes overly formal? In the nude?"

A deep chuckle drifted over. "One of the places we used to sleep was a local theatre. I started learning English by watching enactments of Shakespearean and post-colonial plays. You know those people wrote proper English."

"You're fascinating."

"You're changing the subject."

"It's not my bed."

"You've been sleeping in it for days. Shouldn't it feel familiar already?" His voice had gone low, seductive.

As if he needed to try.

"Kal—"

He went on, not giving her intended protest the light of day. "Think about my hands touching you when the sheets caress your body."

She swallowed. Since they'd already shared the ultimate act of intimacy before, his request wasn't outrageous. Besides, on hot days back home, she slept either naked or in her underwear. She certainly thought about him when she went to bed. Doing the two at the same time? Because he asked? So intimate.

"Will you do the same?" she asked.

"If it's your request."

She caught herself nibbling on her lower lip. "It is."

CHAPTER EIGHTEEN

"Are we going to talk about the elephant in the room?"

Edina blinked at the unexpected question from India. Dinner had ended thirty minutes earlier, and they'd now gathered in the drawing room of Queen Sapphire's lavish personal quarters. Conversation had been free-flowing with Zik's sisters regaling them with tales of their respective new home nations, Wanai and Sudar. Which made India's question, asked during a lull in conversation, seem that much out of the blue.

Queen Sapphire raised an elegant eyebrow. "Elephant, dear? Is everything all right?"

"She means Mr Kalahari Asanti," Isha offered.

The sisters exchanged a look, which suggested they'd already had a discussion about Kal. The thought had Edina's heart skipping beats. What had they talked about?

"What about him?" Zik asked.

"Shouldn't we do something for him? Like throw him a welcome party?"

Edina's heart warmed towards India.

"Isn't that what today's cocktail was about?" her sister asked.

"I'm thinking something more intimate. Just us siblings. He's our brother, and we should get to know him."

"He might be related to us by blood, but he's still an outsider who could have any motive for showing up now."

Zik nodded. "We need to know if we can trust him. I'd have him thoroughly investigated before all the necessary formalities with his oath of allegiance are completed. Zareb agrees with me."

"Of course he does," India replied. "It's his job to be suspicious of everyone. Zareb would have all of us under constant surveillance if he had a choice."

"What makes you think he doesn't?" Isha said.

"Good point," India conceded.

They laughed. Edina listened to the easy banter with a twinge of jealousy. She remembered when she and Barimah had casual chats and laughs. Those had become few and far between since he'd become king. They'd reduce further when she was crowned queen and they'd have to discuss kingdom matters on a regular basis.

"What do you think of all this, Edina?" Isha asked. "Does our new brother strike you as someone with a hidden agenda? I heard you've been working with him on the museum project."

She pushed aside her musings and tried to inject some lightness into her tone. "I think it's safe to assume he can't have any bigger secrets than what's already been revealed."

"True enough."

"We should still make sure," Zik said.

"Agreed," Isha replied.

India shook her head. "You two are so cynical."

"And you are too trusting for your own good."

Their mother raised her hand, cutting off India's response. "Your brother and sister are right, India. We're not saying he's bad, but if he has ulterior motives, we need to find out now. You of all people should appreciate this."

"I do, but I also know what it's like to be the outsider and to be unfairly mistrusted."

"This isn't the same as what you went through."

A pained look crossed India's features. "Isn't it?"

She'd made international news a couple of years ago when her marriage to Prince Majid El-Dansuri of Sudar had ended in tragedy following an accident on the way to their honeymoon. She'd then been inherited by her brother-in-law, Omar. The less known fact, which Zik had briefly mentioned, was that India had initially been a prime suspect in Majid's death. Though it had all worked out for India and Omar, the beginning of their relationship must have been rocky.

"Did anyone else notice there's something … sad in his eyes?"

"He's burying his mother on Saturday," Edina said.

Four pairs of eyes stared at her.

"The king did mention something about that," Queen Sapphire said.

Without waiting for anyone to question how she knew this, she explained.

"He happened to mention it in conversation." While she had the floor, she might as well say it all. "He invited me."

A few seconds elapsed.

"Really?" Isha asked. "Why?"

"The topic of conversation, I guess." She tried to sound casual. As far as they were concerned, she and Kal only had a professional relationship. "We were talking about loss, and I happened to mention my father's passing."

"I think we should all go," India said.

Isha's brows hooked up. "Because?"

"He's our brother, and we must show him what it means to be a Saene."

"Like I said before, we may share blood, but we don't know him well enough to show up uninvited at a private occasion."

"For what it's worth, I agree with India," Edina said. "In Umaasie, we have a saying. 'One shouldn't be left to bear one's grief alone.' Anyone in his shoes could use support at a time like this."

Even if he doesn't know it, she added in her head.

Isha aimed a questioning stare at her. As a lawyer, she must be formidable in the courtroom. Edina didn't flinch. She might be petite, but she didn't cower before anyone—except maybe her mother. Why was Isha so suspicious of Kal, so unwilling to give him a chance?

"I know Kalahari's brother," India said.

Edina's entire focus was riveted on the queen of Sudar. She wouldn't have noticed it if an earthquake occurred right now.

"Foster brother," India corrected. "The man who stood behind him at the reading. Shaka also happens to be friends with Omar, and he did us a favour we could never repay him for."

Her mother looked contemplative for several seconds. "And your gratitude for this favour is such that it extends to his kin?"

"Yes, Mum," India said. "Until he himself proves unworthy of our trust."

That settled it. India was her favourite of the Saene siblings.

"Very well. I shall speak to the king and Queen Zulekha."

"What kind of life has he had, I wonder? What sort of man is he? What would it have been like if he'd grown up with us?"

Isha nodded. "Would he have a bigger stick up his ass than Zareb? Would he be a sensitive soul like Zed? Or would he have given Zik a run for his money with the ladies?"

India snorted. "Doubtful."

"Really, sisters? In front of our guest?" Zik asked, looking mildly embarrassed.

His sisters laughed. Edina shook her head as her own laughter subsided. She liked the dynamic between the siblings. She was happy Kal had reunited with them.

***

Kal had lost count of how long he'd been in the library devouring volumes of material on the history of the Saenes. Mamaa had told him a lot about Bagumi and the royal family. Before he'd started this journey, he'd also read every available material, but some of these documents weren't publicly accessible. As a territory that had escaped colonisation, a lot of Bagumi's history and literature had yet to be unearthed by the rest of the world.

The time hadn't been smooth-reading, though. Every so often, his mind would kick-start with a mental countdown he'd struggle to shove to the background for a few moments but never managed to shut off, making one thing clear. Tonight would be difficult; tomorrow worse. All he could think about was bidding a final farewell to Mamaa.

When a call from Shaka came in, breaking through his thoughts, he stared at the phone for several moments, unwilling to answer. He knew the reason for the call and didn't want the overdose of emotion he suspected would come with it. Shaka would keep calling, though, so he shook off the disinclination to answer and swiped the green icon at the last minute.

He offered no greeting. "Shaka."

"Hello to you, too, brother."

He sighed, knowing Shaka had good intentions for calling.

"You okay?" Shaka asked.

"It's just another day."

"Yeah, sure. It's just the night before Mamaa's birthday."

"You had to go there."

"Normally, I know to leave well enough alone, but you're in the lion's den, and you need to be careful."

Kal sighed "I know."

They talked a little more and agreed on the time Shaka should arrive on Saturday morning before disconnecting.

CHAPTER NINETEEN

Tweeting birds heralded a sunny Bagumian morning, their cheerful songs streaming in mockery of Kalahari's anguish. His chest ached as if his heart had been ripped out of his chest and a piece of lead put in its place. Not a bad thing, he realised, as it allowed him to detach himself and function on autopilot. He'd never make it through today in one piece otherwise.

After a troubled sleep, he'd woken up at dawn and gone for a run. He'd returned to his suite and taken a shower. He'd still had an hour until Shaka's arrival, which he'd whiled away by attending to his emails and other urgent work-related issues.

Presently, he stood in front of the mirror getting dressed. He'd chosen a black kaftan set—a signature Yadira design—handmade by Mamaa. Its suit-style trousers differentiated it from regular kaftan bottoms, but that wasn't the only thing setting this outfit apart. He pulled it on, remembering the day she'd given it to him almost three years ago.

He'd been at the office when she'd called asking him to pass by her place on his way home.

When he'd arrived shortly after six, she'd given him a quick hug and kiss before ushering him into her home studio where she'd laid out the two-piece ensemble. He'd already suspected she'd asked him over in order to make a guinea pig out of him. She'd often delighted in testing out new—sometimes outrageous—concepts on him.

"And here I was thinking you'd asked me here for some fufu and *nkrankra*."

"I have soup, but sadly no fufu," she said. "Go try it on. I'll wait out here."

Proceeding to the dressing room, he inspected the outfit. The trousers were paired with a collared kaftan, layered to give the appearance of a knee-length coat opened to reveal a mid-thigh-long shirt. It had a great fit—structured, yet loose enough to be comfortable—with perfect finishing. The style combined Western, Eastern, and African elements—as to be expected from a Yadira design. Embroidery detail on the cuffs and faux lapels hid Bagumian symbols—another unique aspect of his mother's label.

The clothes fit him perfectly, and he knew immediately it wasn't one of her runway pieces. She'd made this for him. When he found her back in the studio, she stared at him, eyes gleaming with warmth and joy and pride. His heart swelled in response.

"Do you like it, Rahim?"

Of course he did. Not just because it fit him like a glove, but he delighted in seeing the excitement in her eyes. She went into designer mode, inspecting the outfit for non-existent flaws.

"What do you call this?" he asked.

"Silver," she answered.

"I'm guessing the name has to do with the embroidery?"

She nodded. "It's made with silver threading that glitters when the light hits it just right. Like your eyes."

"It's stunning, Mamaa."

Stepping back, she folded her arms and asked him to turn around. He humoured her with a runway rotation and pose, realising too late the trap he'd set for himself.

"When will you model for me again?" she asked.

He sighed. "Mamaa—"

She raised her hands, cutting off his protest. "I know. Just wishful thinking on your mother's part. You were such a natural."

He'd modelled for her before. When she'd been too broke to afford professionals. At sixteen, he'd already hit six feet. Added to his slim frame toned from various physically intense odd jobs he did, he'd apparently been perfect for the role. He'd soon caught the eye of photographers and magazines. He hadn't liked being in the spotlight, so as soon as the label had garnered enough interest, he'd quit to focus on his education and other interests.

"Now you'll have to find a girlfriend so you can wear this to impress her."

Ah, he should've known. He grinned, deciding not to engage. He wouldn't win. "Aren't you supposed to be teaching me to show women there's more to me than pretty clothes?"

"I raised you right, so that's a given."

She rose on tiptoes to kiss his cheek. At five-ten, she was tall for a woman, but she still had to stretch up to compensate for the difference in their heights. He made it easier by meeting her halfway.

"I'll sew you another one," she said. "A nicer one. White brocade fabric with gold threading for your wedding."

"I should have guessed there was a catch." He laughed. "Shouldn't I have a fiancée before you start planning my wedding?"

"Which brings us back to finding you a girlfriend," she said without a smile, clearly opting to ignore his teasing tone. "I'm over fifty. Wishing to see my prince settled down with a good woman and giving me grandchildren is normal."

He hugged her, more to silence her than anything.

She responded with a smile that told him she was on to him. "Now go and change back, and let's have some of that soup you wanted."

A knock at the door yanked him out of the memory.

He dragged in a breath and checked his watch. Right on time. He turned and immediately, his gaze landed on the wooden case now sitting on the cocktail table—inside it, the urn with his mother's ashes. Tearing his eyes away, he headed for the door and wrenched it open.

Shaka stood there, hands on hips, wearing full black, his eyes sharp but sad. "Ready?"

"As I'll ever be."

He left the door open as he went to get the urn.

Like a zombie, he began the long walk to the grotto named for the queen of the king's heart.

"Is she coming?"

Kal cast a glance around, as if expecting Edina to materialise out of thin air.

"She said she would," he answered.

Walking through the stunning grounds, the contrast between the surroundings and his emotional state couldn't be starker. Within him, the pieces of his heart that had survived Mamaa's death were disintegrating. On this day, nature chose to show off.

As they approached the stretch of trees where he'd kissed Edina the other day, he couldn't help thinking about her and how much his mum would've liked her. He shut it out of his mind before the overload of emotions had a chance to break him.

They took a stone-paved pathway, bypassing the grove. As they turned a bend, what met their eyes stopped them in their tracks. Standing there in various shades of black were Edina and the entire Saene family.

"Wow, this family sure knows how to make an appearance," Shaka murmured.

Or cause trouble. If they intended to prevent him from honouring his mother, they'd soon learn that a wounded lion was far more dangerous than a healthy one.

When they reached them, he faced King Ibrahim. "What's going on?"

"We're here to support you, son," he said.

A sudden wave of emotion socked him in the chest. His throat tightened, and his eyes prickled. What the hell was happening to him? He hadn't cried since Mamaa passed, but today, it seemed to be all his eyes wanted to do. He blinked and swallowed.

"You shouldn't have to do this alone," India said quietly.

His hands tightened around the handles of the wooden case. He nodded, focusing on conquering the urge to break down.

"Thank you," he said.

"I'll lead the way," the king said and began to walk.

Kal and Shaka followed, and the rest of the family fell in step.

Ibrahim led them to a nearby stream. The monarch had already brought Kal here yesterday, so he knew they'd be crossing it. Large stones lay in the stream, their flattened tops protruding several inches above the surface of the water.

"Are we crossing?" one of the princesses asked.

Ibrahim stepped onto the first stone, eliminating the need for an answer. They arrived at a clearing in front of a small cave whose entrance was partially covered with overgrown bougainvillea—the grotto named after the queen of the king's heart, his mother had called it. Kal intended to ask the king for the meaning or at least the real name.

"Let's sit," the head of the Saene family said, motioning to some stone benches on one side.

Kal placed the case on the grass in front of them but remained standing. He'd planned on simply entering the cave and spreading the ashes, perhaps spending a few minutes saying goodbye. That plan flew out the window as he looked into their faces.

"Eleven months ago, I lost my best friend," he said. "Some sons would be embarrassed to call their mother their best friend, but mine was. For the first ten years of my life, Mamaa and I were all each other had. She did everything possible to keep me safe and to give me shelter. Her love was all-encompassing and fierce."

As he said the next thing, he looked at the man who'd been a significant part of his mother's life despite his absence. "She died because of love."

For some reason, when he said "love," his eyes sought out Edina. She sat in a regal pose, legs crossed at the ankles as if she were seated on a throne rather than a garden bench. Nature or fate or fucking karma hadn't let up, because she was breath-taking in her black lace boubou and her hair concealed under a black silk scarf. No jewellery.

A stirring in his chest yanked him back. Best to hand over the floor to someone else while he regained composure.

"I'm sure Shaka has a few words he'd like to say."

He left centre-stage and sat as Shaka gave his eulogy. Kal drifted in and out of concentration with various memories of his mother until King Ibrahim came forward.

He didn't want to feel anything for the monarch, and yet, as the man stood unspeaking, eyes looking less vibrant than before today, something tugged at his heart.

"I loved Yara," Ibrahim said.

Whatever had pulled at Kal's heart congealed into something hostile. Was this man for real? He couldn't help glancing at his wives and children, noting their varying expressions of surprise. Despite the general bad taste in his mouth, he had to hand it to the king. He excelled at playing the part of the grieving ... lover?

"She was kind-hearted and selfless, which I'm sure Kalahari and Shaka would testify to." He paused again, as if weighing his words. "She also had a way of talking to you and making you feel like you could do anything, be anyone."

A lump grew in Kal's throat. Mamaa was exactly that. No matter how dire their situation, she'd always made him feel special, calling him her handsome prince and telling him he'd one day rub shoulders with kings. She'd been so convincing, he'd had no choice than to believe.

King Ibrahim sighed. "It breaks my heart that I never got to see her again before she was taken from this Earth."

Taken? Kal stifled a bitter laugh at the base of his throat. She took matters into her own hands. Because of King Ibrahim! He had no right to stand there talking as if he cared about Mamaa when he'd driven her out of his life and her home. He remembered her letters. From the tone of some of them, if she hadn't ended her own life, she might have sunk into a depression that would have slowly drained her of her essence. Also because of him.

He fought to keep his mouth shut, a losing battle. Suddenly, he felt a touch on his hand. He turned sharply and realised Shaka sat next to him. He breathed in, bringing his emotions under control as the king finished off.

"Kalahari and Shaka need to do the next part." Facing them, he added, "It's time for us to spread the ashes."

His body tensed. *Us?* Once again, Shaka intervened with a gentle prod. Kal calmed himself as he returned his gaze to Ibrahim.

Kal's heart tightened. Having to share his and Mamaa's last moments together with the monarch grated. Yet, a part of him felt pity for the man. He'd been watching King Ibrahim closely during the eulogies. The man looked tired, seemed to stand less tall than he usually did. Something within him conceded Ibrahim's grief could—on some level—be genuine, but allowing the king to be a part of this moment would grant him closure he didn't deserve.

Another part of him knew this was exactly how Mamaa would have wanted it. In honour of her, he reined in his anger. Besides, although Ibrahim had brought him around yesterday, they hadn't entered the cave, so on second thought, having the king lead them in was probably the best course of action.

As they rose, so did the rest of the family.

Queen Zulekha approached him first. "I'm sorry for your loss, Kal. I'm glad she had two sons who loved her as you do."

"Thank you, Queen Zulekha."

The queen's height matched Mamaa's, as did her words spoken with the same composed strength he'd often seen in his mother.

Queen Sapphire followed with brief words of condolence, her eyes filled with sympathy that made his heart ache even more. His half-brothers came next, shaking his hand. Isha followed her brothers' example, but to his surprise, India embraced him and Shaka, even exchanging a word with his brother. He knew Shaka was acquainted with her husband, King Omar of Sudar, but he hadn't realised Shaka and India knew each other. Interesting that his brother hadn't said anything.

Once the tone had been set by her sister, a pregnant Amira also hugged him. When Edina stepped in front of him, his heart began to beat rapidly in anticipation of feeling her body against his. Which example would she follow?

"From everything that's been said, I can tell your mother was a lovely person," she said.

"She was."

Rising on tiptoes, she wrapped her arms loosely around his shoulders. In this instance, he lost the battle with temptation and allowed his arms to enfold her for a brief moment. It was all the time he could allow himself. Otherwise, he wouldn't want to let go.

"I'm sorry you lost her."

"Thank you."

The family departed, leaving Kal, Shaka, and King Ibrahim.

"It's time," Shaka said.

At the entrance, Ibrahim lit an old-fashioned lamp. They descended a couple of meters, and the grotto opened up. At least half the space was filled with water. He guessed the stream they'd crossed passed through here. He set down the case, opened it, lifted the urn, and placed it at the edge of the stream. Unscrewing the lid, he took a handful of ashes. Gently, he unfisted his hand and watched the waters carry the ashes off.

"I'll forever miss you, Mamaa."

Shaka and Ibrahim did the same. They continued taking turns until the urn stood empty. As he watched the stream take away the last bit of Mamaa he had, his tears finally fell. He looked away, unwilling to let either Shaka or Ibrahim see him cry. Yet, he couldn't stop his eyes from expressing the emotions he'd denied his heart all this time.

Arms enfolded him.

"Let it out, my boy," King Ibrahim murmured.

Weeping, it turned out, sapped a person's energy. He found none to prise out of the older man's hold. Suddenly, he was a little boy again, crying himself to sleep because he'd discovered the meaning of the word 'bastard.'

Mamaa had found him in tears once and had wrapped him in her loving arms, whispering assurances of the existence of a father and filling his impressionable head with stories of the man's bravery, his important job that prevented him from being with them. All he'd wanted was one day, one opportunity to show them all he wasn't lying, that he, too, had a dad.

The more he'd tried to convince them, the more jeers he got. Eventually, hope had turned into hate as he'd come to the cruel realisation that they'd been right. Finding himself in this position, being held by his father, the man he'd learnt to despise, thrust him in unfamiliar territory—consumed with hatred, yet somehow grasping at hope.

He didn't know how long he'd allowed himself to be embraced while his tears flowed. He now sat on the dusty floor of the cave, his heart still in pieces. Shaka had left some moments earlier, but Ibrahim had stayed. Neither had spoken since his brother's departure.

Kal inspected his surroundings. It was larger than the small entrance suggested. The atmosphere was cool, and perhaps because of the stream, the air had a damp smell. A small hole at the top provided limited light, but Ibrahim's torch made up for the rest. As caves went, this was ordinary. So obviously, whatever made it special to Mamaa had everything to do with the man she'd loved.

"I haven't thought about this place in years." The king finally broke the silence. "What did your mother tell you about it?"

"Nothing," Kal replied. "Just that she wanted her ashes to be spread here."

"It used to be a shrine centuries ago, but not since the palace was established here. Nobody ever comes to this spot. Even back then. People feared spirits of the uprooted deities haunted the place. As a young boy, the stories didn't scare me. I'd come here whenever I wanted to think, attracted by the idea of communing with the gods." He had the faraway look of a man who'd drifted into memories. "This is where your mother first told me she loved me."

Kal didn't want to listen to the king talk about Mamaa. Yet, he couldn't bring himself to tell Ibrahim to shut up. Perhaps, deep down, a part of him needed to hear the monarch talk about his mother, needed to be convinced she hadn't wasted her love.

"Thank you for bringing her back, Kalahari."

He looked at Ibrahim. "I did it to fulfil her wishes."

Ibrahim nodded and fell silent again.

"The queen of the king's heart," Kal said. "What does that mean?"

Ibrahim's lips lifted slightly. "Haven't you guessed already?"

"I don't like guessing games," Kal replied.

Ibrahim stood. "Come, son. I'll show you something."

He led Kal to one wall of the cave, brushed off the dust on a spot until an engraving in the wall became apparent. Kal bent forward, shining the torch against the image etched into the rock.

He frowned. "An eye?"

"E. Y. E." Ibrahim smiled. "The old Bagumese spelling of Ibrahim starts with an 'e.' Ebrahim and Yara for Eternity. What we felt for each other transcended life itself."

Kal looked sharply at the king. Was his position shaking? Did he truly believe the king had cared for Mamaa? Impossible!

"You put in a lot of effort into making her fall for you."

"You still doubt your mother's place in my heart."

"You keep saying you loved her, and I'm tempted to believe you did. In your own way. What I don't get is why you'd exile a woman you claimed to love."

"I let her go for her protection."

A darkness rose in him. The nerve of the man—painting himself as some kind of hero.

"How were you protecting her when she had to work multiple jobs to keep us clothed and fed?" he asked through gritted teeth, barely keeping his tone in check. "Where was your protection when she nearly lost her son, *your* son, because she had no money to take him to the hospital when he convulsed from malaria?"

Relief swept through him at the surprise on the king's face. He'd been bursting at the seams, keeping himself in check all these years—even more so after finally meeting him. And today was the worst day for anyone to test his patience.

"I'm sorry I wasn't in your life."

The king's face was grave, his words spoken in a low tone, echoing with sincerity. It was like a pinprick to the dam he'd built to contain his emotions—the hopes and dreams he'd had as a child; the disappointment and façade of indifference he carried around as a teen; the resentment that had finally settled in his gut, fuelling his actions as an adult.

"I loved you. A man I'd never met. I made up stories in my head about your reasons for not being with us. Then I hated you. So much." A humourless laugh escaped him. "Did you even try to find her? Keep her safe even if you never intended her to be anything more than your plaything?"

"I wasn't playing games with Yara."

"Your actions don't support your words, Your Majesty."

King Ibrahim sighed. "I made a vow to Queen Zulekha. She had to give her blessing for any new wife I took. With your mother, no matter what I did or said, she wouldn't—"

Kal bit back a curse. "You chose her over my mother."

He didn't know why the revelation cut as deeply as it did. Had the king truly intended on marrying Mamaa? He wasn't surprised by the queen's decision. A woman of her station and privilege would be affronted by her husband's marriage to a servant. Her opinion of Mamaa didn't matter, anyway. Now, he had all the information needed to remember she was as much an enemy as her husband.

He'd been a fool thinking today of all days, he'd get any kind of closure, that Ibrahim would somehow emerge worthy of exoneration. He'd been wrong.

"I thought you had ultimate power, but the truth is you're a weak man."

"You won't understand—"

"Then explain it to me!"

Seconds ticked off as indecision played across the man's face. Kal held his breath, waiting. For what, he didn't know.

The other man shook his head, sighing. "I can't tell you more than I already have."

"Then hear me, Your Majesty," he spat out. "The doctors ruled her death as an accident, but they didn't have all the facts. Despite your rejection, she never stopped loving you, never allowed a better man to care for her the way she deserved. Eventually, she couldn't handle the heartache!"

The king looked like he'd been sucker-punched, but Kal didn't waste pity on him.

"You said she was taken away from us? She committed suicide."

"Oh, Yara, what did you do?" The old man's voice came out sounding broken.

"Let me be absolutely clear to you, old man. I hold you responsible for her death."

Ibrahim reached out, but Kal pulled away.

"You chose your beloved kingdom over her. Over us. That was your first mistake." Something in his brain tried to put the brakes on his anger, warning him to examine his words before speaking further, but he was way past caring. "Your second mistake was putting me in a position to take it away from you."

Ibrahim's eyes widened. He opened his mouth, about to say something. Kal raised a hand to cut off whatever lame excuse the man intended to give. He'd heard enough of his lies.

"Kalahari, you're grieving. You don't know what you're saying."

"You don't know anything about me," he retorted. "This conversation is over."

CHAPTER TWENTY

Mamaa's funeral hadn't given Kalahari the closure he'd hoped for. It had been two days now, and he still couldn't shake off the sense of foreboding brewing in his gut. His angry outburst at the king testified to his slipping composure. His run this morning hadn't helped, so after returning early from the company's temporary offices in Darusa, he'd found himself back on the trail trying to clear his head and exhaust his body.

His anger at the king notwithstanding, the royal family's support at his mother's funeral had meant more to him than they'd ever know, but he couldn't simply abandon his plans. Not until he was certain they were clean.

Returning from his run, his muscles were stretched and aching. He hoped it meant his mind would be weary enough to welcome sleep. Otherwise, he might not be able to stop himself from dialling Edina's number at inappropriate hours. No sense in depriving them both of a good night's rest.

The sounds of laughter interrupted his thoughts. A child's mingled with an adult's—two adults, he amended when he heard the distinct tones of a man and a woman. He stopped walking, needing, for some reason, to absorb it. Without any conscious decision, he started towards it, stopping short when he found the source. Prince Zediah and his family occupied a section of the palace gardens where a play obstacle course had been set up.

He'd known Zediah had a wife and two children, but those details hadn't been important to his cause, so he hadn't paid them much attention. His gaze zoned in on the little boy. Judging from his somewhat jumpy steps, he had to be between two and three. His father cheered him on while his mother held up a phone, obviously recording it all. The other child—an infant, if he recalled correctly—was nowhere in sight.

The three made a striking set—the boy with his toffee complexion and soft curly dark brown hair, a combination of his father's African and his mother's Indo-Mauritian and Indian roots. That wasn't what kept him glued to the spot, though.

A twinge pierced his chest, causing him to wince and suck in a deep breath. For the longest time, this was all he'd ever wanted—to have a dad. Emotions constricted his throat, forcing him to swallow. The shadows he no longer allowed to take up space in his head began to close in on him.

He turned to leave, but that plan went horribly wrong when his foot caught on a pavement block that jutted out a fraction more than the others in the pathway.

His quick reflexes kicked in, but with nothing close to grab, he landed on his hands push-up style. The laughter had ceased, he noted and cursed under a breath. There went any hopes of not getting caught encroaching on their privacy.

Nothing to do now but to own it. He stood and found them staring at him. The child squealed and clapped as if Kal's fall had been some sort of entertainment. He supposed it would excite a two-year-old. He'd never dealt with toddlers. The children he interacted with through Kalahari's Kids were several years older. Younger ones normally came with a parent or older sibling, whom it made more sense to deal with.

"Forgive me," he said. "I didn't mean to intrude."

"Not at all." Zediah scooped up his son, grinning.

The pair approached him while the child's mother lagged behind, tapping at her phone screen. He guessed she was sending the new footage of her son's prowess to friends and family.

"Care to join us?" Zediah asked in a tone tinged with a British accent.

Kal shook his head, looking down at his sweat-stained T-shirt. "I'm not dressed for the occasion."

Despite the excuse, he found himself stepping forward, stopping a couple of metres in front of them. The child babbled something that garnered a smile from his father.

"Do you know who this is?" the prince said in a most indulgent voice. "This is your uncle, Kalahari."

As though he understood his dad, the boy raised his arms, reaching towards Kal.

"Ank Kah."

"That's right. Uncle Kal." Meeting his gaze, the proud father said, "And this little adventurer is Nour."

It took a moment for Kal's mind to snap back into gear. He'd been stuck on the word "Uncle," uttered with an ease of manner that made his heartbeat stumble. While their shared DNA made the tag factual, he hadn't expected Zediah to admit it with such facility.

He forced a smile to hide the emotions. "Hello, Nour."

"Next time, you can meet his sister, Alayna. The nanny just took her in for her nap."

The kid gave him a toothy grin, pointing at his arm. "Moshu."

Zed laughed. "Yes, Uncle Kal has muscles."

"Yah," Nour said, raising one arm in what he supposed counted as flexing.

Kal had no idea why he mimicked the gesture, but his actions were rewarded with a delighted squeal. This time, he didn't have to force his smile. The child's mother joined them then, having stowed away her phone. Her unsmiling expression told Kal she didn't appreciate him appealing to her child's inner macho-man. She must be the kind of mother who wanted to raise a well-rounded child. Perhaps he should have worn a regular T-shirt instead of a tank top which left his biceps on display. He'd only factored in the heat and humidity when picking out his running attire.

The moment Nour noticed his mother, he tipped towards her. She seemed to have expected it, since she easily caught him and hoisted him on her hip with one arm around his back.

"I guess we know where his allegiance lies," Zediah said with a chuckle. "You haven't officially met my wife, Rio."

He inclined his head. "My pleasure to meet you, Rio. I'm Kalahari, or Kal."

"Pleased to meet you, too, Kal." She maintained his gaze as if searching for something, then shook her head. "I'm sorry for staring. It's just, you and Switz have such similar eyes."

He frowned. "Switz?"

"Oh. I mean, Zed. I'm still not used to calling him by his given name."

"It's an alias I used while living in London."

Kal nodded in understanding. At the same time, Nour started to fidget, reaching for Rio's ponytail, which she deftly tossed over her other shoulder.

"You're getting hungry, aren't you?" she cooed at the boy who looked at her as if the sun and moon shone from her eyes. "But you can't eat Mummy's hair, love."

"He must be tired, too," Zediah said.

Rio nodded, cupping the boy's face and kissing one chubby cheek.

"I better get some food into him before he naps." She turned to Kal. "Very nice meeting you. I hope we have a chance to get better acquainted soon."

"Likewise," he replied.

"Bye-bye, Ank Kah," Nour said as they walked away.

Kal waved back. "Bye, Nour."

He and Zediah watched them until they'd reached a picnic set-up he hadn't previously noticed.

"He's lucky to have a father who's there for him," he said.

"Believe me, I'm the lucky one," Zediah replied. "I missed out on the first nine months of his life. Now that he's a part of mine, I can't imagine not having him. Both of them, and Alayna, too."

Kal dared not think about the woman he couldn't imagine his life without. Not right now. Not in front of Zediah. Seeing the look of contentment in the prince's eyes, hearing it in his voice, intensified his determination to have Edina. Damn the cost.

"I guess it's a two-way street," he said. "Take it from the guy who grew up without a father."

"The funny thing is, there was a time I couldn't wait to get away from mine," Zediah replied with an embarrassed sort of laugh. "From ours, I should say."

Kal didn't bother telling him how he truly felt about the king, but he couldn't squelch his curiosity. Perhaps it had something to do with the prince's unexpectedly welcoming persona.

"Was he not a good father?"

He didn't know why he hoped Zediah would condemn King Ibrahim. Would that be enough to confirm Kal hadn't missed much by not having the man in his life? Did it justify his reason for being in Bagumi? He gave himself a mental shake. He couldn't start second-guessing his actions now.

Zediah grew thoughtful. "He was there when it mattered, I guess, but Baba has always been a king first. Everything else came second. He was full of high, often rigid, expectations. The others took it in their stride, but I found the obligations of royalty stifling. I needed to pave my own path, figure out who I was besides being a prince of Bagumi."

A snort sounded from him before he could stop it.

"I know what you're thinking," Zediah said. "Only a privileged bloke would say that."

"You don't agree?" Kal responded.

"Maybe you're right." The other man shrugged. "But trying to accept it led to panic attacks I wouldn't wish on anyone."

Kal's brows hooked up. He understood the prince's sentiments. Unlike Zediah, though, he'd gladly transfer his troubles with sleep onto someone deserving of those nightmares.

"And now, you're thinking why the hell is he telling me all of this." Zediah chuckled. "I figured I could trust a guy who didn't get all macho to compensate for falling flat on his face."

Zediah's playful tone reminded Kal of Shaka's penchant for poking fun at him, though the prince managed to be slightly less annoying.

"I wouldn't call that falling on my face."

Zediah waved a hand, his expression still jovial. "Don't worry, you look as princely as any of my other brothers."

Kal was about to say something when Rio's voice drew his attention. She moved a spoon in a gliding motion while making aeroplane sounds.

Nour shrieked, opening wide when the spoon reached his mouth.

"If the plane came out, then he doesn't want to eat," Zediah said.

Kal nodded. "I better let you get back to your family."

He'd taken a couple of steps when Zediah called out. "Hey, Kal."

He turned.

"We—the siblings, I mean—sometimes gather in one of the lounges in the evenings just to hang out. It's the best time to get to know us."

Just like with Nour, he didn't have to force his smile. He liked Zediah's energy.

"Noted."

"Welcome to the family. If you ever feel smothered by all this ..." He waved a hand in a wide circular motion. "Remember to be true to yourself. Live your truth."

"Is that what you did?" he asked. "Rejecting the marriage contract between Bagumi and Barakat?"

Zediah seemed marginally surprised by the question but didn't appear put off. "In a sense. I couldn't go through with it after learning about Nour and reconnecting with Rio. I had to live my truth, and Bilkiss did the same."

"Well, enjoy your evening," he said.

The prince nodded before turning towards his family.

Kal glanced back at Nour, taking measured breaths to release the vise tightening around his chest. He didn't remember much of his life at that age, but he'd certainly never had the luxury of refusing to eat anything his mother fed him. He tried not to begrudge the boy for having a childhood the polar opposite of his own.

He'd never dared imagine himself as a dad. The concept of fatherhood often filled him with a sense of animosity. Yet, the sight of Zediah with Rio and Nour brought yearning to his heart.

As he began to walk away, the image in his head transformed. There was no question about the identity of his children's mother. He could see it clearly—him and Edina making fools of themselves and loving every minute of it while trying to persuade their child to eat.

She'd be a great mum, he had no doubt. With her, he needn't worry about failing his kids as his father had failed him.

The thought stopped him in his tracks. While he'd never planned to have children, he'd never actively doubted his abilities as a dad. After all, many of the kids his foundation rescued from the streets saw him as a sort of father figure.

All this time, that role had been satisfactory. Now, a different truth confronted him. Kalahari's Kids wasn't enough. For every family he helped, he remained on the outside. As with the Saenes.

He let the realisation sink in. He wanted what he'd always yearned for—a place to belong. A family.

Was it possible he'd subconsciously used his work with the foundation to hide his fears? Would there be no end to the pain King Ibrahim could inflict? Learning the monarch hadn't been the kind of father he'd wished for, even to his other children, sealed the man's fate in his mind. He didn't deserve redemption.

A more important thought assailed him—one he didn't want to consider. After he'd exacted revenge on the man, would Kal be beyond salvation in Edina's eyes?

CHAPTER TWENTY-ONE

Over the past few days, Kalahari had been splitting his time between working in his suite and the new office he'd been assigned at the palace. This was where he held his civics lessons, as he liked to call the sessions with a special attaché tasked with preparing him for his appearance before the king makers in a week's time.

He had seven days to demonstrate equal knowledge about Bagumi's culture, economy, and politics as any of the Saenes. If he passed muster, he'd have a couple more weeks after to present his vision for the future of the kingdom. He'd even have to swear an oath of allegiance to the Crown.

How had his plan to make King Ibrahim suffer come to this?

The answer was simple.

Edina.

He'd do this and more if it meant being with her.

He hadn't anticipated enjoying the lessons. He'd expected a classroom style set-up where he'd be force-fed patriotic mumbo jumbo. Instead, he'd received a candid education on the kingdom—covering both the positive and negative—from a man who was knowledgeable and passionate about good governance.

He was an older gentleman whom everyone referred to as Efo, meaning uncle in the Ghanaian language, Ewe. With Ghana being the current headquarters of Asanti Holdings, the commonality had made for an excellent conversation starter the first day they'd met. In addition to theory, Efo had set up virtual meetings with influential government personalities as well as visits to a couple of historical and industrial sites.

It had been several gruelling days of this, which he'd normally take in stride. Today, though, he was anxious to get into central Darusa for lunch with Edina. The past few days had been nothing short of perfection. Their nightly calls relaxed him. He liked to think it did the same for her. He couldn't wait to get her alone so he could hold and kiss her.

After Efo had left his office, Kal grabbed his phone and headed for the door. He'd barely taken a step when it opened, admitting a palace staff in livery.

"Announcing the High Queen, Her Majesty Queen Zulekha," the man said, positioning himself just inside the entrance.

Before Kal could process what was happening, the first queen of Bagumi swept in. She oozed a certain regal elegance having nothing to do with the flowing purple lace boubou or her grey-streaked dreadlocks which were scooped up in a stylish do adorned with tribal beads. Even in her late fifties, she had the kind of beauty that would turn heads.

"You must bow before the queen."

A voice drew his attention to the two ladies-in-waiting behind.

Their identical reproachful looks didn't reveal who'd spoken. He didn't care what they thought of him, though. He hadn't come to Bagumi seeking anyone's approval. Nevertheless, he dipped his head to the queen, which seemed to appease her henchmen. The queen herself maintained an impassive expression.

"Privacy," she said.

In no time, the other three filed out, leaving just the two of them.

He waited for her to make the next move. After all, *she* had sought him out. It wasn't exactly a surprise. After the king had shocked him by allowing his appearance before the king makers, he should have known a visit from the first queen of Bagumi was imminent. She probably meant to dissuade him from pursuing this line of action.

"My husband has asked me to speak on your behalf," she stated.

He blinked, sure he hadn't heard correctly. The king continued to surprise him at each turn, keeping him guessing. He didn't like it.

"Why would he do that?"

She flicked a hand towards a chair. The command didn't need verbalisation. Still reeling from her declaration, he forgot to remind her *she'd* come to his office. In any case, she'd probably just tell him this was her house.

He stepped back and lowered himself onto the armchair she'd indicated. His mistake became immediately apparent when she admitted herself farther into the room but didn't sit. With him seated and her standing, she'd assumed a position of power. Nothing to do but make the best of it.

Feigning composure, he sat back and adjusted the embroidered sleeve of his navy kaftan. The gesture allowed him to steal a glance at his watch. He grimaced. Looked like he'd be late for lunch, and he couldn't even send a message.

"Do you have somewhere better to be, Mr Asanti?"

He dropped his arm and gave her his attention. "Forgive me, Your Majesty."

She gave a snort of laughter. "So she passed that on to you. She picked it from me, you know."

"Pardon?"

"Your mother," she replied. "Saying 'I'm sorry' can be construed as an admission of guilt. 'Forgive me' fools people into thinking you're apologising, when in truth you're demanding their pardon even when you feel no remorse."

The corners of his lips ticked upwards in concession. "I apologise. I didn't mean to be impudent."

Seemingly satisfied with his response, she cast her gaze around the room in an unhurried manner. Impatience would have had the best of him if he didn't know exactly what she was doing. Mamaa had employed this tactic many times, and he'd learnt it from her. Had she picked this, too, from the queen?

He shook himself. Though Mamaa had seemed unique, this was probably a trait all mothers possessed. He decided to focus on the queen's many non-Mamaa-like attributes. He couldn't afford to get emotional now.

But it was too late. The silent ache in his chest smarted. Was he ever going to get used to not having her around?

"To answer your question," the queen was saying. "The king loves all his children, and that sentiment applies to you."

"He barely knows me."

"If ever you have children, you'll understand a parent's love isn't constrained by time, rules, or even reason." Her demeanour remained unruffled. "However, we need to uphold the provisions of our constitution, which means your claim of intent must be adequately supported. This is where I come in. My word is indisputable, and as such will solidify your case."

"I have the ring," he argued.

"Which could get lost."

His eyes narrowed. Was that a threat?

"With all due respect, Your Majesty, I don't trust you."

"You don't have to, but this isn't a fight you'll easily win on your own."

"I'm willing to take my chances."

"Don't be a fool, Mr Asanti. This kingdom has survived—thrived—for centuries without you and will continue to do so whether you become an official member or not."

He wanted to counter that, but she made an excellent point. No one would dream of contesting her testimony. What he didn't understand was why she'd want to help when she'd been the reason King

Ibrahim and Mamaa never married. Assuming the king had been telling the truth.

The concept of his beautiful mother not being first place for any man proved unconscionable. He was firmly in the exclusivity club. He couldn't imagine sharing his woman with another man. By the same token, he'd never expect his woman to be okay with sharing him.

He returned his focus to the queen. The sooner he appeased her, the quicker he could get to Edina.

She sat down on a sofa opposite him with a not-quite-smug expression. "So, Mr Asanti, do you have somewhere more important to be than right here convincing me you deserve my help?"

He reminded himself why he was doing this. *For Edina.* She was worth a change in his plans. Which meant he couldn't reject the queen's support no matter how much he'd like to tell her where to put it. He had no alternative than to hear her out.

"No," he eventually said.

"Probably untrue, but a wise answer," she replied. "Why don't you start by telling me what you're really after?"

"I could ask you the same," he said. "Why would you want to help a man you barely know and possibly risk the throne of Bagumi?"

"I think you know you'll never be named Crown Prince as long as there's already a legitimate candidate," she replied. "Besides, I wouldn't be here if I thought the throne was your real goal."

His heart clenched, but he couldn't afford to lose the reins on his temper right now. He breathed in deeply, holding it for a few seconds before letting it out. Outwardly, he hooked his brows to convey detached curiosity. "What if you're wrong?"

"I don't think I am." She surveyed him for a long moment. Was she trying to read his mind? "This entire situation has happened because my son abdicated. If events had happened differently thirty-two years ago, you would've been next in line by order of birth."

"So you feel guilty?"

Her shoulders stiffened a fraction, but she showed no other sign of vexation. To her credit, she seemed to consider his question.

"The consequences have turned out to be more than I'd have expected, but I stand by the decisions I made." She shook her head. "If Yara had stayed, she'd have destroyed this family."

He bolted up.

"I don't care who you are." Remembering the potential witnesses on the other side of the door, he fought to keep his voice low. Not much he could do about his rising anger, though. "I won't have anyone denigrate her when she isn't here to defend herself."

She didn't flinch or react to his sudden outburst. "What about the truth? Will you listen to that?"

Breath rushing out as though he'd just run a race, he narrowed his eyes at her. "What truth?"

"This might not be something you want to know about your parents."

"What truth?" He enunciated each word as his voice dropped menacingly low.

Once again, Queen Zulekha pointed to the chair—the one he'd just vacated. He stared at it for a long moment, trying to decide whether he wanted to hear this. What would he gain by putting himself in a position to be mentally manipulated by her? How could he not, though? He had too many questions about his mother and not enough answers. But was he rational enough to discern the truth in whatever she intended to say about Mamaa? Caution and curiosity warred for dominance. After a moment, he sat back down.

"Don't say I didn't warn you, Mr Asanti."

He didn't respond, giving her space to speak while bracing himself.

"Yara had a power she didn't seem to be aware of. When she walked into a room, people noticed." A faraway look claimed her eyes. "She was my junior lady-in-waiting, but when I had Zawadi, it became clear how good she was with him. At times, even I couldn't calm him, but the moment Yara picked him up, he'd stop crying."

He released the breath that had hitched in his throat in anticipation of the worst. Tension in his muscles began to relax.

"I promoted her to Governess. I'd had a difficult birth. It took months before I could connect with my child. I relied heavily on her. Ibrahim wanted to spend all his free time with his son. His heir. In a sense, it's my fault they started an affair. I put her in his path."

She looked at him, and he saw regret in her gaze. He had no words.

"History will report my marriage to Ibrahim as a political alliance, but I married for love. I fell for him from the moment we met."

He frowned at the shift in conversation. She continued her speech before he had a chance to say anything.

"My father warned me about offering my heart to a man who didn't give his in return. I was young and confident I could win him over, if not with my love then with my counsel and support as a political strategist. Eventually, I had to accept what my father had cautioned me about, but I made Ibrahim promise to get my permission if he ever wanted to take another wife." She gave a snort. "I had no idea he'd take me up on it, let alone choose my son's governess."

So, the king hadn't lied.

"But you refused," he stated. "Because what? You saw her as someone beneath you?"

She shook her head. "Yara was beneath no one. I was hurt, but it had nothing to do with arrogance. I was jealous."

He frowned. "Jealous?"

"Have you heard the saying if you want a mother to love you, love her children?" She didn't wait for an answer. "Watching Yara with Zawadi … it seemed my heart took it literally."

He sat up. What the hell?

"I'd developed feelings for Yara, and she preferred my husband. When he met Sapphire and wanted to marry her, I agreed. Maybe because I wanted to punish Yara for choosing Ibrahim."

She was reeling him in. He could see that, but for the life of him, he couldn't prevent her ensnarement.

"The night of their wedding, I found Yara weeping in one of the conservatories. She looked as broken as I felt." She held his gaze, and he saw the rawness of her emotions. "Just that one night, I needed her, and she needed—"

"Stop." The word grated against his throat. "Please, stop."

He couldn't mask his own shock and disbelief.

"She—" His voice cracked. "Both of you?"

Several seconds passed as he tried to wrap his mind around the revelation.

"Yara was like the sun. She brightened everything around her, but you can't get too close to the sun without getting incinerated."

The anger he tried to hold in check ignited in his chest, lending a sharp edge to his voice.

"The two of you couldn't control yourselves around her, and somehow, it was her fault?"

"It's not that simple," she replied. "Being with her drove a wedge between us. We had fights over her, but we didn't want to lose her."

He bit back an expletive.

"Are you seriously going to sit there and try to convince me neither of you drove her away? That my mother upped and left of her own volition without a penny to her name?"

"She told me she'd met someone she was going to marry."

"But you knew that had to be a lie."

A beat passed.

"Most likely, someone found out about Yara and the king and threatened to expose them. I believe she was already expecting you by then and did what any mother would do. Protect her child."

He drew in a long breath, rolling his fingers into tight fists. It helped when his emotions were spiralling. He held the queen's gaze. She didn't turn away or school her expression, leading him to conclude she was telling the truth.

He didn't know what to do with that. Or the fact that Mamaa had this whole other side of her he never knew about. Questions spilled into his head, each toppling over the other, crowding his mind.

He stood and stomped to the window, shut his eyes and focused his energy on breathing, breaking down the thoughts and compartmentalising them until he began to feel a degree of equanimity.

Did he believe her? Had the revelation tainted his memory of Mamaa?

No. If anything, he appreciated her more. What bravery it must have taken to extricate herself from the emotional pull the king and queen must have represented for her.

To protect me.

The queen's presence beside him wrenched him out of the mental cocoon. He didn't look at her, instead choosing to train an unseeing gaze outside the window.

"Did you try to find her?" When she didn't reply, he shook his head in disgust. "You both claim to love her, and yet, it was so easy to let her go."

"I had a child who needed me to think of, but don't think for a second that letting her go was easy."

His throat tightened, and he swallowed. His eyes burnt. He squeezed them tight. He needed this conversation to end before he completely lost it.

"The past is set in stone, but perhaps we can change the future," she said. "Will you accept my help?"

He shook his head, not knowing what he was rejecting. At some point, he'd begun questioning his reason for coming to Bagumi. When the Saenes had shown up to support him to say goodbye to Mamaa, he'd been humbled.

He realised his mistake now. These people were master manipulators. To them, love was a weapon meant to bend people to their wills. They'd abused Mamaa's love, used and discarded her like she meant less than nothing. Now they thought they could buy their absolution with pointless declarations of love? It may have worked on Mamaa, because she'd loved them. It wouldn't work on him.

What had the queen hoped to gain from telling him this story? His sympathy? Understanding? Forgiveness? Where was the apology in all this? The audacity of privilege!

"Your actions robbed me of my birth right." He had no idea how he kept his voice even. "I want it back."

"Then I'll help you get it."

"Including succession to the throne," he added. "It's the only way you can begin to make up for everything you took from me."

CHAPTER TWENTY-TWO

Edina couldn't make her pulse slow down even if she possessed superpowers. It had been nearly a week since her first night call with Kal. They'd spoken every night since, trading stories and getting to know each other. They hadn't made love yet, though, which accounted for her constant sexual frustration. She couldn't wait to be intimate with him again.

In a few days, Kal would've had his say before the panel tasked with deciding his fate in the Saene line of succession. She had no doubt he'd ace the test.

Him jumping through all those hoops for her sake made her love him so much, it would've scared her if she didn't know he was also doing this for himself on some level. He'd told her about feeling untethered growing up. Now, he'd have a father and seven siblings.

She couldn't be happier for him. After missing out on so much, not only had he reunited with his family, but he'd finally have an official place among them.

She didn't care about his status, but her people might. A place in the Bagumian line of succession would negate any objection her mother and brother could raise against their union.

As soon as she returned to Umaasie, she'd inform Barimah and her mother. And it would be official. She and Kal would finally be together.

She was headed out for her lunch date with him when her phone rang. His name flashing across the screen made her pulse race.

"Hi," she answered the call.

"Edina."

She frowned at the tortured way her name sounded.

"Kal, are you okay?"

"No."

Alarm shot through her.

"What happened?"

"Long story."

"Where are you?"

"Office. Palace."

Kal wasn't a chatty person, though he'd been different with her, which made his one- and two-word responses more alarming.

"I'm coming," she said.

"Don't—"

She'd already hung up.

***

Kalahari lost track of time while pacing and flexing his fists, focused on releasing the rage raking through him. He'd barely managed to contain it while the queen had been here. Alone now, he was losing the battle. All he could see was Mamaa's face every time he'd caught her with that distant look in her eyes when she'd thought no one was looking ...

What had they done to her that her very spirit seemed to have remained here?

His heart ached from breaking for the woman whose only crime had been to open herself up to love. He scoffed. Love. Was that what love did? Had he doomed himself the same fate as his mother by falling for a royal? He'd already reached the point where he'd do anything just to see her happy. If she did to him what *they* had done to Mamaa ...

No. He couldn't go there.

"Kal?"

The sound of his name pierced through his muddled thoughts, and he turned. His initial elation at the sight of her immediately gave way to distress and a sense of foreboding. He was in no state to be near her. His emotions were not yet under control.

Concern filled her eyes as their gazes locked. "Are you okay?"

Her voice was like a sprinkle of water on the fire of his anger. The thing about water was that it could put out small flames, but inside him, an inferno raged, and those fed off water.

"You shouldn't have come," he said, a clear edge in his voice, before turning away again.

His brushoff didn't have the desired effect. She didn't leave him alone to sort out his emotions. The click of the door shutting heralded her approaching footsteps. A moment later, she placed a hand on his shoulder. Her warm touch nearly put a chink in his armour, but he steeled himself. He needed to avoid emotions of any kind right now.

After several moments of not acknowledging her, she spoke.

"Look at me, Kal."

His jaw tightened with his disinclination to do as she asked, but he'd never been able to ignore a direct request from her. Reluctantly, he angled his face to meet her gaze.

"What happened?" she asked.

She had that damned look in her eyes. The one that made him talk. He didn't want to unleash what lay within him when he'd barely had time to sort it out for himself.

"Queen Zulekha came to see me," he found himself saying.

Her brows hooked up. "And?"

"The king asked her to testify on my behalf. She'll confirm the king intended to marry my mother."

He told her about his conversation with the queen, leaving nothing out. When he was done, she just stared at him, choosing silence over platitudes. He wasn't done, anyway.

"They used her, then discarded her as if she didn't qualify to clean the dirt off the bottom of their shoes, and yet, her heart remained here," he spat out. "With them."

That last part hit him hardest. How could she have yearned to be back here after the way they'd treated her? Were the good times worth the disgrace and heartbreak? Memories of his night with Edina flooded his mind. He'd do anything for more nights with her ... for a life with her. But he'd never set his expectations as a noose around his child's neck.

A different set of memories poured in—far less pleasant ones.

"When I was ten, I got into a fight with a guy for calling me a bastard." The words grated against his throat. "Except on the streets of Abidjan, the slang translated into 'son of a whore,' because only that kind of a woman would get impregnated by a man who wouldn't offer her marriage."

Her horrified gasp accompanied a sympathetic expression. Against reason, a shadow of the shame he'd experienced that day wafted over him.

"When I got home, she beat me with a cane." His heart clenched. This was something he'd rather forget. "She'd warned me time and time again never to get into fights, because I couldn't afford to incur scars. 'Know how to fight,' she'd often say, 'but never throw the first punch.' It didn't matter that, in this case, I was defending her honour. I didn't first seek a non-violent solution as she'd taught me."

He swallowed down the sandpapery sensation in his throat. She squeezed his upper arm, reminding him she was still touching him. He stepped away, breaking the connection. He didn't want to see pity in her eyes.

"That's when I discovered, whoever my father was, he had a whole other family, and the only way I could be a part of his life was to be damn near perfect."

Mamaa's words echoed in his head. "When you meet your father, you mustn't look out of place."

"Do you know what it does to a boy to spend his childhood getting his ass whipped into shape, so he could someday measure up to some mysterious other family? Imagine my disappointment at finding them so unworthy."

"I'm sorry you had to go through all that, Kal," she said. "Your anger is justified, but—"

He faced her again. "But?"

"Anger also poisons your heart," she said. "Holding on to it for all this time. Aren't you tired?"

He was. God, he was, but it was immaterial. At the end of the day, Mamaa was gone, and King Ibrahim was the root cause. For a moment, he'd let the man's charisma sway him. No more. He had to pay. Even at the cost of blackening his own soul.

"Have you stopped to consider that the only reason you're this angry is because you actually like them? You're hurting, I get it, but does it mean they're beyond forgiveness? Think of your own peace and healing."

"I'm beyond healing, and I don't want peace." He couldn't hold her wide-eyed gaze. "I want chaos. You were right the other day. I came to Bagumi with an agenda. I wanted to punish the king for his abandonment. I wanted him to feel some of the pain and uncertainty I grew up with because of him. This process ends with me taking the throne or destroying it."

"You can't mean that."

"Oh, I do."

"Then you leave me no choice."

His heart hammered a furious rhythm against his ribcage.

"What are you going to do? Run along and tell them?"

She shook her head. "I don't think I'll need to. You're a one-man army. You can't win."

Her words hit him like a slap on the face. "Good to know how little faith you have in me."

"I do. I have faith you can rise above the need to inflict pain on others." She threw her hands up in a gesture of resignation. "Because if you can't forgive them ..."

She paused as if reluctant to finish the sentence.

He narrowed his eyes, and the sense of foreboding he'd felt when she first entered returned. "Then what?"

"I'm sorry, Kal. I can't be with a man who's incapable of forgiveness."

He recoiled from her. "You're taking their side?"

What had he expected? She might as well have stuck a jagged knife in his chest.

"There are no sides here. They may not be perfect, but they're your family."

"I had a family. She's gone."

"No one can ever replace your mum, but think of all you're gaining. A father."

"I had a father for five years. That was enough."

"Brothers."

"I've got one I'm happy with."

"What about sisters, huh?"

Did she think this was a game?

"The queens—"

"Don't make up for the mother I lost. The one they took away from me!"

Silence followed his outburst. A look crossed her face.

"What?" he snapped. She didn't respond. "Speak."

"Don't you think you're being a bit unfair? Your mother made a choice. She isn't completely blameless—"

Rage detonated within him.

"Get out," he gritted.

Her startled eyes stared between his face and the arm he'd flung towards the door.

"Kal, I'm sorry. I didn't mean to—"

"You're just like them, aren't you?" he spat out. "Royal. Privileged. Selfish."

She flinched, the hurt in her eyes unbridled. Any other day, her pain would've turned him to putty. Now, he saw things more clearly.

"You're even better at this game than they are," he continued. "All that time bemoaning your fate. You knew I'd offer myself without you asking."

"This is not a game."

"You can play innocent all you want, but we both know the truth." A harsh laugh broke out of him. "Innocence is part of your act."

Her lips parted with a gasp, her eyes widening with recognition of her words from their first conversation.

"That's right, Honey Eyes. I remember every word you've said to me."

He'd fallen hard for her, and what had she done? She'd just stood on her pedestal and watched him fall on his sword for her. Anything to be with her.

"I've been such a fool for not seeing it. Here I am making this huge sacrifice to be worthy of you. Meanwhile, you haven't even once said you love me."

"You know I do," she cried.

No. All he knew was love had made him weak. Mindless. He'd willingly put himself in a position to be crushed by her. If she did, he'd never survive it. The prospect scared the hell out of him. Better cut the cord before it got to that.

"Do I?" he retorted. "Have you told the other guy you no longer intend to marry him?"

She started to say something then stopped.

"Of course, you haven't."

"It's not a conversation one has over the phone. Not with my brother."

"Or you're keeping him as back-up in case this—" he pointed between them, "—doesn't work out. Forgive me for insinuating myself into your life. I'll save you the trouble of having to play me against him."

"Don't do this, Kal. Don't push me away."

Her lips quivered, and he thought she'd cry. For a moment, remorse assaulted him. Until she fortified herself with a series of rapid blinks and a deep inhalation.

Five seconds. That was all it took for her to acclimatise to the notion of being rid of him. He should have known better than to fall for a royal.

"Go." Did she hear the strain in his voice? "Marry the suitor you have lined up and be happy. Or not. I don't care."

Once again, he gave her his back, unwilling to see the pity and indifference he'd surely find in her eyes. After a moment, the door clicked shut, signalling the end of them—a relationship that soared without really taking off. Even with eyes shut tight, moisture managed to escape in a thin line down his cheek.

***

Edina moved away from the door, flames of shame burning her face as she propelled her body forward on leaden feet. Her heart which, a mere hour earlier, had danced with hope and exhilaration now lay shattered in her chest. She should have known better than to believe love could alter her fate.

Love? For a moment, she'd allowed her heart to override reason, and look what that got her.

Her vision swam in a pool of tears that eventually fell in hot rivulets down her cheeks when she blinked. She tried to unsee the hate in his eyes, unhear the venom in his voice when he'd used his words to cut her. He couldn't have inflicted more pain if he'd walked her blindfolded to a cliff and tossed her over the edge.

He'd accused her of not saying the words, but neither had he. She hadn't complained. To her, his actions had been enough testament to what lay in his heart. Or so she'd thought. Clearly, she'd mistaken what had been going on between her and Kal.

Having her heart ripped out and trampled on was the price she had to pay for that grave error in judgement.

She swiped the tears away, increasing her pace in hopes of getting to her suite before bumping into anyone.

In this regard, fate smiled at her. Once inside her bedroom, she started packing her things. She had just a couple of days of her two-week visit left, anyway. Every outstanding task could be handled remotely from Umaasie.

A princess doesn't run from her problems.

One of her mother's mantras popped into her head, but she squashed it. She wasn't running away. For once, she was running towards something. Someone. Her soon-to-be fiancé.

The last thought caused her heart to squeeze painfully. She winced but ignored it. She'd always been prepared to sacrifice her happiness, after all.

CHAPTER TWENTY-THREE

"And now, the international news. He grew up on the streets of Accra, Abidjan, and Niamey, but today, he fights for the right to sit on the throne of the kingdom of Bagumi. Financier Kalahari Asanti—"

"Could you turn that off, please?" Edina said to the chauffeur and did a mental "la la la la la la" for the few seconds it took for her request to be fulfilled.

A week had passed since she'd returned to Umaasie, and the pain of losing Kal hadn't receded. She'd kept a low profile, filling up her calendar with charity events in addition to her regular work at the museum. She spent most evenings at home alone or with her family.

None of her endeavours had expunged him from her mind. It didn't help that he was on the news every other day, and trending on social media. Although, eighty percent of the posts were from women who thought he was—quote, hot and wanted to have his babies, unquote.

Their last encounter played on a reel in her head. The things he'd accused her of ...

Snapping of fingers pulled her out of the deluge of memories. She inhaled sharply, bringing her focus back to the concerned eyes of her best friend. They were in her official vehicle on their way to visit victims of a local market fire that had occurred during Edina's trip to Bagumi. As she'd promised her brother, she was taking on more official public duties.

"He really did a number on you this time, didn't he?" Jamila said. "Before, you always broke into smiles when you spaced out, but now, you're just broken."

She tried to smile, and somehow failed at the simple gesture. "I guess he broke me."

"Oh, honey," Jamila said, squeezing her hand. "I'm sorry it didn't work out. Last week when we spoke, you sounded so happy and hopeful."

"Hope crashed and burnt." She let out a heavy breath and stared out the window. "It's better I found out now than later. Next week, I'll be officially engaged, and Kalahari will be in the past where he belongs."

"I can't believe you're going through with the engagement ceremony without first meeting the man," Jamila said.

"What's the point? Besides, we've met before."

"And you thought he was arrogant."

"I fell in love, Jami. I allowed a man to ensnare my heart and mislead me with his sweet words. I can't do it again, so this arrangement is exactly what I need."

The ache in her heart proved love wasn't always the best thing. Having it felt great, but losing it hurt too much. She hadn't even had Kal's love, and yet, being without him felt like she had a lance lodged permanently in her chest.

Every now and then, she found herself remembering their conversations, his magical touch, his enchanting words, his chivalrous actions. Each time he'd said her name, it had sounded like music … How could he fake all that?

She grimaced, shutting out the thoughts. She'd promised not to do this, not to analyse their time together.

A few seconds elapsed before her best friend spoke again. "If I ever meet Kalahari, I'll punch him."

Her mind conjured up images of his hard, muscular body. "Don't. You'll hurt yourself."

"Are you really worried about me getting hurt or him?"

Despite herself, Edina laughed. Relief spread across her friend's face as she joined in.

After a moment, Edina sighed.

"*Bahalia* invited me to dinner tonight," she said, referencing their secret couple name for her brother Barimah and his wife, Mahalia. "You should come and insulate me against all the love they're going to be displaying."

"Sorry, but I already have plans."

The sparkle in the other woman's eyes and the smile she tried to conceal by biting on her lower lip were a dead giveaway.

Edina gasped. "Is it a date?"

Jamila nodded, giving her a wide grin. "I didn't say anything, because I didn't know how you'd feel about it."

"Happy. Maybe I can live vicariously through you." She grinned. "Who is it, and how long have you been seeing him? Tell me everything."

As her friend recounted highlights of her budding new romance, Edina immersed herself in the conversation which, for a moment, helped her forgot about her pain.

***

"Best of luck, today, Mr Asanti."

Kal snapped out of his thoughts and focused on the man who'd prepared him for his first appearance before the kingmakers.

"Thank you, Efo."

He was supposed to be happy. In an hour, he'd have his moment, one he'd fought for. Yet, his heart might as well be a block of lead.

"If I may speak freely, sir." The older man seemed to hesitate.

"Go ahead, Efo."

"It will be nice to have an active member of the royal house who's experienced the plight of some of the least privileged of our society."

He nodded. "I appreciate the thought."

"You have supporters, you know." The man smiled. "My daughter tells me hashtag *I heart Prince Kalahari* is trending."

"I'm not a prince," he replied, and the echo of a conversation nearly nine months ago twisted the knife in his heart. He tapped his chest and added, "Not yet, but thank your daughter for me."

Efo bowed. As he exited, a uniformed staff walked in and announced the king. The monarch entered alone, closing the door behind him.

Kal began to rise. "Your Majesty."

With a raised hand, the older man stopped him. "Sit."

He resumed his seat. The older man's gaze trailed from his head to his hands clasped together on the desk and back up.

"How are you feeling?" he asked.

He quirked a brow. "Good."

"It's all right to admit you're nervous."

His smile was conciliatory. "I'm not used to baring my emotions."

"You're part of a family now. Get used to it."

Family.

Edina's words came back to haunt him. "They're your family ... Think of all you're gaining."

He'd thrown it in her face and lashed out at her for being honest. He'd had more than a week to live with the consequences of his stupidity.

He'd come to his senses soon after sending her out of his office with his cruelty. It had already been too late. He'd tried to find her, but she hadn't been in her suite. Assuming she'd detoured somewhere to lick the wounds he'd inflicted on her, he'd returned an hour later, then another hour after that. Three times, he'd knocked on her door, hoping to finally see her and fix things. Each time, his hopes had been dashed by the resounding silence.

Late afternoon the following day, he'd learnt the truth. She'd left Bagumi that morning. She'd done exactly what he'd asked—she'd returned home to marry someone else. And he had only himself to blame.

He almost wished Shaka were here to tease and give him grief. Then he'd have an outlet for the agony ripping through him. Unfortunately, Shaka had left Bagumi for an undercover job after deeming Kal's life to be out of imminent danger. He had no one to confide in, no one to lift the gloom overshadowing him.

"I have something for you." The king's voice brought him out of his thoughts. The older man thrust a photograph in Kal's direction. "It's a picture of your mother. I thought you'd like to have it before going in."

Doing his best to maintain a neutral expression, he took the photo and looked at it.

"You didn't say it was of the two of you." He studied it for a long moment. From the background, it had to have been taken somewhere on the palace grounds. Probably near the grotto. "You both looked so young."

"We were."

"She always said I looked like my father."

He hated to admit it, but he saw the resemblance. He had King Ibrahim's eye shape and thick brows.

"You're full of energy and passion, just like her."

A few seconds elapsed while he looked at the photo again, noticing their intertwined fingers and the sparkle in Mamaa's eyes. He'd never seen her like that. The king also looked happy, though without knowing him well, it was difficult to tell whether he'd been in love.

"Why did you keep it?"

"It's the only thing I have of her beside my memories."

A smile crept onto his lips in reflex. He liked hearing Ibrahim talk about Mamaa like this. The one good thing resulting from Edina's departure was the deep soul-searching it had forced him to do. It had forced him to acknowledge the truth of her words. Every single thing she'd said had been right.

He'd spent time with the king over the past week. It had started out as penance for his actions, and maybe a search for salvation. He might never understand the choices Ibrahim had made all those years ago, but he'd begun to accept there may have been some genuine emotions on the king's side. He had no idea if the older man knew about Mamaa and the first queen, but he'd decided it wasn't his truth to tell.

For now, he chose to focus on the only parent he had left. Knowing his mother occupied some part of Ibrahim's heart and memories somehow made up for the fact that she'd never stopped loving him. It wasn't a fairy-tale situation by any stretch, but it was something. He'd even started softening to the idea of being the son of King Ibrahim Saene.

***

Kalahari was ushered into a much smaller replica of the throne room where the DNA results had been read. Before him sat the king, the two queens, and the six chieftains who held his future in Bagumi in their hands—five men and one woman, who being the longest-serving among them, had two votes.

He bowed before them and waited to be spoken to.

"Mr Asanti, welcome to the court of king makers," the woman spoke. "You have the floor. Make it count."

He knew exactly what he intended saying. He'd gone over it in his head so many times, he could recite it in his sleep—all the reasons he deserved to be admitted into the inner sanctum of the House of Saene, every advantage he brought to the table.

Finally, he'd push an emotional agenda—securing a legacy for his future children so they never felt untethered like he had.

He scoffed at the thought. What children? In his adamant pursuit of vengeance, he'd lost the only woman he wanted to have children with. And for what? A title? He'd never wanted one to begin with. It had all been for her. A family? It had no meaning. The Saenes had a shared history, their lives interconnected. Even if he ever truly became a part of that, it would take time.

He'd give it all up for a chance to be with Edina. As far as he knew, she wasn't married yet. Maybe—

"Anytime you're ready," one of the other chieftains said.

For some reason, his gaze sought Queen Zulekha. She gave a slight nod.

"I'm sorry." He grimaced, unable to believe what he was about to do. "I have to go."

Their surprised expressions mirrored his own.

"What's the meaning of this?" a third king maker spoke up. "Do you think you can waste our time?"

King Ibrahim raised a hand, and they all fell silent. "What's going on, Kalahari?"

"There's no point in winning the battle and losing the war."

With those words, hope sparked in his heart.

"You understand, Mr Asanti, if you walk away now, you won't get a second chance," the female chieftain said.

He nodded, smiling for the first time in over a week. "I apologise for wasting your time."

He turned to leave and hoped to God he wasn't too late.

CHAPTER TWENTY-FOUR

Edina stared at her reflection in the mirror, thinking about the events that had culminated in this moment—her engagement day. Except for those brief moments in Bagumi when she'd imagined marrying Kal, she'd always approached the idea of her marriage with a level-headedness that came from knowing she was destined to enter a marriage of state.

For her look, she'd chosen a mix of cultures— her form-fitting *kaba* and mermaid-cut skirt made from hand-woven kente cloth from northern Ghana, a hand-spurned Nigerian *aso-oke* headtie—both custom-made. She accessorised with diamonds from Botswana, North African henna designs on her hands and feet, and bridal face art from East Africa.

Outwardly, she looked flawless. Inside, however, lay a chasm that threatened to swallow her whole. This was her reality to live with for the rest of her life. To be forewarned is to be forearmed, right? She could do this. She took in a deep breath and exhaled slowly.

A knock on her door brought her out of her thoughts. It would be either her mother or her best friend.

"Come in," she answered.

Queen Nataizia and Jamila paused for a few seconds.

"Wow," Jamila said.

"You look breath-taking, my child," her mother said.

Edina forced her lips to curve up. "Is it time?"

"I know this is a marriage of state, but could you please look a little more excited?" the queen said. "If you can't be happy for yourself, think of the people of this kingdom and all the well wishes you've received already. A princess is always gracious."

"Even when it hurts," Jamila, who'd come to sit by Edina, muttered under her breath, making Edina crack a real smile despite the truth in the remark.

"That's more like it." Queen Nataizia came to sit on the other side of her and cupped her face, her touch delicate so as not to mess Edina's make-up. "I promise you, we've done our due diligence. Your husband-to-be is a perfect gentleman. Once you learn what pleases him and vice versa, you'll enjoy every blessing marriage has to offer."

"Thank you, Mum."

"Now let's go. Your cousins and aunties are waiting outside to escort you."

***

Gathered in the palace courtyard were Edina's immediate and extended family and a few close friends of the family to witness the traditional engagement ceremony where the groom and his family came to formally ask for her hand in marriage.

This was a private affair—immediate and extended family with close friends. She wouldn't be so lucky when it came to the wedding, which would follow in three months. Queen Nataizia wanted nothing less than a grand fairy-tale affair for her only daughter. Edina knew how to choose her battles, so she'd given in, thankful for the low-key traditional engagement ceremony.

She stood in front of her brother, mother, and family elders seated at the end of the rectangular space farthest from the entrance. The rest of the family sat in rows on the left and right.

As custom demanded, the groom and his family were outside, waiting to be invited in.

Her brother presided over the event, explaining the purpose of the gathering as demanded by custom, after which he handed over to their oldest maternal uncle, deemed the head of the Dampare clan.

Her uncle addressed her formally. "Your Royal Highness, *Owoahene* Princess Edina Masira Dampare. We're gathered here to witness the asking of your hand in marriage. Do you consent to this?"

Her heart jumped. Discomfort wound around her chest like a vise. *I can do this.* After all, this was just the engagement. Until the wedding was finalised, she could change her mind. But she wouldn't, though. Her marriage would end the threat of Zoraya and enable her to focus on her other motive.

Despite his rejection, Kalahari's brazen actions in Bagumi had inspired her. Along with the decision to marry, she'd also resolved to launch a campaign against the marriage stipulation for the Princess of the Crown. No longer would she simply accept the rules or quietly rebel against them. She was born to be a queen, not a prisoner!

She breathed in and out before returning her mind to the ceremony. "Yes, Uncle, I do."

The question was repeated twice before her uncle turned to the king. "Your Majesty, *Owoahene* accepts this engagement ceremony."

Nodding, Barimah gave an order. "Let the visitors in."

Edina faced the entrance as the palace guards opened the gates. The groom's party entered, led by a troupe of energetic, colourfully attired drummers and dancers. She wondered how comfortable they were wearing nose masks while exerting themselves. *Odd.* They looked West African, but not Ashanti. Next came a group of eight men and women bearing gifts for the bride. Behind them ...

She gasped. Her hand flew to her mouth, her eyes widening.

Kal?

Was she daydreaming again? She squeezed her eyes shut and opened them again. He still approached in his gallant gait, wearing a gorgeous white and gold full-length kaftan that made him look even taller. Their gazes caught. She could feel the heat from his stare even at that distance, and her knees weakened. She saved herself by shifting her focus to his entourage.

Directly behind him were Shaka and Princes Zawadi, Azikiwe, Zediah, and Zareb; then came their sisters Isha and India. Following them were their significant others—Danai, Rio, and Malika. She supposed Amira's pregnancy had prevented her and her husband, Jake, from travelling.

Behind them were the two queens and King Ibrahim. She wouldn't have expected King Ibrahim to travel given his age and heart condition. But a wedding wasn't complete without the father of the groom. Her heart pounded. Was this really happening?

Suddenly, the dejection sitting heavily on her shoulders since the moment she'd agreed to the engagement began to disappear. She held her breath, afraid breathing might cause the scene unfolding before her to disappear.

Her heart nearly flatlined when Kal stopped in front of her and his essence surrounded her. Eventually, she began to accept this might not be happening in her head.

"I'm sorry it took me so long to come to you," he said.

His voice flowed over her, around her, like salve, soothing the ache in her chest.

She shook her head. This couldn't be real. The thought hit her like a zap of electric current. If it were, then what happened to the real groom? Had he changed his mind and forgotten to do the honourable deed of informing her beforehand? So much for him being a true gentleman.

"You're welcome to my court, members of the Royal House of Saene," Barimah said.

Her brother didn't appear surprised at all, Edina noted. She turned to look at her mother and Jamila. None of their expressions mirrored her shock. Were they all in on this? How long had they been plotting things behind her back?

Her face heated up, her heart thumped. How had Kal managed to influence her family and friends to take part in this ... whatever this was from all the way in Bagumi?

"What's going on?" she demanded.

"My name is Kalahari Asanti, son of Ibrahim Aziz Saene, King of Bagumi," he announced.

She couldn't help noting the absence of the disdain or hate he'd had just a couple of weeks ago. Did that mean he'd finally forgiven his father? If so, then she was happy for both father and son.

"What's your mission in Umaasie, Kalahari Asanti, son of King Ibrahim Saene of Bagumi?" Barimah asked.

"I'm here to ask for the hand of Princess Edina in marriage, if she'll have me."

His declaration resulted in a ripple of excitement within her. She clamped down on it, remembering how things had ended the last time she'd allowed herself to fall for his charms. She wouldn't let him humiliate her like that again, especially not in front of her family and friends.

He looked at her. "Will you have me as your husband, *Owoahene*?"

God, the way he said her title made it sound like a song ...

No. He did not get to waltz in here looking like a damned god and expect her to fall for his charms.

She jutted her chin up, calling up all the courage she could muster. "I will not."

A hush fell over the hall. A barely perceptible widening of his eyes was his only visible reaction—perhaps a realisation that she hadn't said yes. The silence was thick and palpable. She didn't dare look at anyone lest she lose her confidence.

Kal faced her, giving her a full-frontal assault of his magnetism. She noticed then the dark circles under his eyes, the slight downturn of his sensuous mouth. Her hands itched to touch his face, to soothe the shadows around his eyes, to soften the stiff outline of his lips.

Under his intense stare, her gaze faltered.

"Do you love me, Edina?"

Silence met his audacious question, and she realised despite her bravado, he still held the aces.

"Can we do this in private?" she asked.

"No," he said. "I want your family and mine to witness this moment, so there are no doubts in anyone's mind when our conversation ends."

A shiver ran up her spine. He'd given her the boot the last time they'd seen each other. Was he here to finish the job? She squared her shoulders, held her head high. Whatever he had up his sleeve, she won't let him win. After all, this was Umaasie, and here, she was held in higher regard than him.

"What happened to my groom-to-be? What did you do to him?"

"We merely reached an agreement."

"What kind of agreement?" she asked. "Did you pay him off?"

When he didn't respond, her anger flared. "Tell me, Kal. How much was I worth? Is this some twisted ploy to prove you wield power over my emotions?"

"You're making an erroneous assumption."

She laughed. "You know what? Thank you for showing me the kind of value you put on me. I don't have anything to say to you."

As she turned to leave, he caught her hand. She jerked her arm, but he didn't release her.

"*I* have something to say to you. Will you at least listen?"

She stared at him for a few seconds. His touch had turned her legs to jelly. She didn't trust them to carry her out of there, so for now, she had no choice but to remain rooted to the spot where she stood. She nodded.

"It figures that I'd fall for a princess," he said.

She frowned, taken aback. "Excuse me?"

"I feel like a complete idiot after everything I've said about royals. You showed me a side of royals I hadn't known. You're more than a princess to me. You're the woman who'd give up her happiness for her country, who'd risk her life to save a stranger's child. You're a beautiful soul that's linked with mine."

He took a knee, and gasps echoed around them.

"What are you doing?" she asked.

He continued to hold her hand. "Edina Masira Dampare, I'm madly, deeply, hopelessly in love with you. You've had my soul since the day we met. My heart beats for you alone. Every breath I've taken since you left has been like a spear in my heart."

"Don't you mean since you threw me out?"

"I was a fool for everything I said to you."

Edina gaped at him. One second, they were arguing, and the next, he was declaring his undying love. She couldn't decide which was real. Tears brimmed in her eyes. She blinked rapidly to get rid of them, but a drop fell down her cheek. With her free hand, she swiped it off.

"If you're going to doubt me," he continued "Let it not be about my love for you."

"Why are you doing this?"

"I realise I'm going about this all wrong." He placed her hand on his chest. "Don't listen to my words. Hear my heart. The power you said I wield over you, you wield the same power over me."

His eyes shone with sincerity, though his expression became despondent.

"If you reject me, Honey Eyes, it would devastate me. I'm not saying this to guilt an acceptance out of you or force your hand. It's meant to show I'm not afraid to let you see my weakness, because I'll also be there when you need me to be strong for you."

She stared at him, unable to force her voice out of the vise gripping her throat.

He released her hand. "Whatever decision you make today, I'll accept it. If you tell me to leave, I'll go and never return. So I'm going to ask you again. Do you love me?"

She stared into the dark depths of his eyes, and her heart filled to overflowing. More tears flowed. She loved him more than life itself. She yearned to say yes, but something held her back.

"You hurt me, Kal. You were in pain, and you lashed out at me."

"I've regretted my actions every minute since. I'm sorry, Edina. Give me a chance to spend the rest of my life making it up to you."

The gathering watched, enthralled. She remained silent, swallowed trying to regain her voice.

Kal remained on his knee waiting for her response. It pleased her. There were a few men who'd genuflect before their women even in apology, but most would do so in the privacy of their chambers. Only a man of substance would feel no shame in publicly humbling himself like this. Certainly, not a prince; even if said woman was a princess.

She knelt before him, smiling. "I love you, Kal. With my whole heart."

"Then put me out of this misery and say you'll accept me as your husband."

Joy expanded within her, filling her until she couldn't stop laughing through the moisture streaming down her face. She nodded.

"Say the words, Goddess. Let there be no doubt in anyone's mind."

"Yes, Kalahari Ibrahim Asanti. I want you to be my husband, the father of my children, and the ruler of my heart."

Cheers erupted around them.

He cupped her face and pulled her in for a kiss. The moment their lips touched, everything receded to the background. She was lost in the moment, lost in him, and yet, somehow, found herself. Joy swelled within her, breathing life back into her heart.

"I missed you," he said when the kiss ended.

"Me, too."

He enfolded her in an embrace, and she wrapped her arms tightly around him. Now that he'd returned, she never wanted to let him go.

"I can't wait for us to be alone, my love," he whispered in her ear. "I hope your room has thick walls, because this time, I mean to hear you scream my name."

She sucked in a breath as his warm breath caressed her skin.

"Would you like that, my queen?"

She smiled. "More than anything, my king."

THE END

Empi Baryeh

Thank you for reading The Illegitimate Prince by Empi Baryeh. If you enjoyed this story, support the author by leaving a review at the site of purchase.

ROYAL HOUSE OF SAENE

THE PRINCESSES:

His Defiant Princess by Nana Prah
His Inherited Princess by Empi Baryeh
His Captive Princess by Kiru Taye

THE PRINCES:

The Torn Prince by Zee Monodee
The Resolute Prince by Nana Prah
The Tainted Prince by Kiru Taye
The Illegitimate Prince by Empi Baryeh
The Future King by Kiru Taye

OTHER BOOKS BY LOVE AFRICA PRESS

Fading Face by Jonah Igwe

Inside Out by Emem Bassey

Forever and a Day by O.L. Obonna

Screwdriver by Kiru Taye

CONNECT WITH US

Facebook.com/LoveAfricaPress

Twitter.com/LoveAfricaPress

Instagram.com/LoveAfricaPress

www.loveafricapress.com